HE WAS ABOUT TO BETRAY HIS OATH!

RODNEY SEARCY

Copyright © 2015 Rodney Searcy
All rights reserved
First Edition

PAGE PUBLISHING, INC.
New York, NY

First originally published by Page Publishing, Inc. 2015

ISBN 978-1-68213-361-3 (pbk)
ISBN 978-1-68213-362-0 (digital)

Printed in the United States of America

TABLE CONTENTS

Introduction..5
Chapter 1...7
Chapter 2..15
Chapter 3..21
Chapter 4..28
Chapter 5..36
Chapter 6..41
Chapter 7..52
Chapter 8..59
Chapter 9..67
Chapter 10..85
Chapter 11..102

INTRODUCTION

This explosive novel centers on a US Drug Enforcement agent, but when world events from the past connect with the present, Agent Thomas Allen soon discovers that his present stumbles into the past. Agent Thomas Allen works for the Drug Enforcement Agency. When Tom is assigned to a new assignment to uncover a drug smuggling operation in the New England area, Tom soon discovers that the woman that he has to arrest becomes the woman that he falls in love with. He then has to make a decision if his love for her and the world events from the past are enough to convince Tom if he should betray the oath that he has sworn to in order for them to live in their future.

CHAPTER 1

The Beginning

The sky was completely blue, and there were birds in the trees chirping. The temperature was sixty-three degrees. The snow that was on the ground had started to melt. It was a Monday afternoon, and the streets were filled with shoppers. Wilhelm Strausvon was in the midst of all the commotion.

"Watch out for that horse manure!" his friend Albert yelled when the two boys had started to cross the street.

The year was 1923. Germany was in economic ruins after World War I had ended in 1918. The Treaty of Versailles had put the country into a financial depression. The people of Germany found life to be unbearable. The two boys had just finished school for the day, but on this spring afternoon they were out seeking for mischief.

"What does it say?" Wilhelm asked. Albert was reaching for the piece of paper that had been nailed to the wooden pole. "It says Adolf Hitler will be giving a speech for the National Socialist Party at the Munich Knights Hall next Friday at 2:00 p.m." Albert crumbled the paper, and he threw it on the ground. The man who was hanging them up witnessed what the two boys were doing. He yelled at them, "Get away from there." Albert and Wilhelm ran down the sidewalk.

"I'm hungry lets go get something to eat?" Albert said. Okay Wilhelm replied! The two boys start to walk in the direction of the vendors, they were selling goods. "Let's steal some fruit?" Wilhelm said. "You keep him busy Albert, I'll grab some Pears." Suddenly, a huge hand grabs Wilhelm by the neck! "Okay you bastard put them back," the voice said.

Wilhelm reached into his coat pocket, and he pulled out two pears. "How old are you son," the Man had asked. Ten, Wilhelm replied, "you boys run along now, before I have you thrown into the Brig!" The two boys ran as fast as they could, and they we're laughing, while they ran. They had started to walk home, Albert was moving out of the country.

"Albert, where are you moving to? I don't know Wilhelm, my father won't tell me! I'm going to miss you Albert. You know Wilhelm if we ever meet again in our lifetime, I hope that we will still be friends, because I love you like a brother." The two boys continued to walk until they reached Albert's house, they both embraced each other and Said; Goodbye!

Wilhelm was walking home from Albert's house. He had to walk up several large hills because his house was in a little valley. The sun was shining brightly on his face when he reached the top of the hill. Wilhelm had slipped and fell; that's when he saw him. "Come here, you little bastard, you can't outrun me!" his father yelled.

Wilhelm had started to run, but soon his father had caught up to him. He grabbed Wilhelm by the collar. He then slapped him across his face. "Not one word to your mother about this. Do you understand? Promise me!"

"I promise," Wilhelm replied. He then started to cry.

"The day you break this promise, boy, is the day God will throw you in hell."

Wilhelm and his dad started to walk to their house. His mother was preparing dinner. She told him to wash up, then Wilhelm went upstairs to the bathroom, and he washed his hands. "I hate my father," he said while he looked at himself in the mirror. Wilhelm was thinking that he couldn't wait until he grew up. Wilhelm wanted to get back at all the people who had hurt him.

Hermann Goering was born in the year 1893 during World War I. He had served in the German Air Force. In 1918 after the death of his squadron leader, a young Hermann Goering was called upon to lead his squadron of pilots. Hermann soon learned that he could command and receive respect from his fellow air force comrades. This single event had set the stage for Hermann to become one of the world's most influential people. He would change the course of history.

The year was 1921. Hermann was headed to the city of Berlin. He wanted to visit the Berlin Art Museum, where he loved to spend hours walking through the museum halls. He would occasionally stop to gaze at some of the world's finest art collections in Germany. Suddenly, he had noticed a man standing near his beloved painting of Fraulein Eva Vondenberg. "She was a gorgeous woman," Hermann said. "She sure was," replied the gentleman that he was speaking with. "My name is Hermann Goering." He reached out his hand. "Adolf Hitler," replied the man. The two men started to shake hands, and they began to embrace each other.

The two men started walking together. They would occasionally stop to gaze at more art. They kept on talking, and soon the two men discovered that they had a lot in common. Hermann and Adolf were discussing their memories of World War I, when they had served in the German military. They were now both concerned with the problems that were facing Germany. Banks closing, unemployment, higher government taxes. The two men had decided to join the National Socialist Movement. Soon after joining, Adolf had become the party's spokesperson.

"Gentlemen, I give you Adolf Hitler," Hermann Goering announced. The applause erupted like the sound of thunder inside the Munich Knights Hall. Adolf approached the podium and shook hands with Hermann. Adolf put both of his hands on the podium. He then stared at the audience. When the applause started to subside, he turned his face and looked at some of the party members. Staring back out at the audience, he then cleared his throat. He then adjusted the microphone. There was now a silence in the auditorium. Adolf again cleared his throat. He then looked at the front row of people and fumbled with his stack of notes. He cleared his throat again as he stared out into the audience. There was now complete silence.

"Gentlemen," Adolf said. He adjusted the microphone, and with a soft voice, he went on to say, "Germany is in ruins. Our leaders have failed to see that our people go hungry. Our women and children walk the streets wearing no clothes!" His voice started to get louder. He raised his fist back and forth in front of his face. "Our men have no jobs, our economy is in ruins, your country is the laughingstock of the world. I tell you this because it's true, and it's all our enemies' fault. The Treaty of Versailles must be abolished." He clutched his fist in the air. He then yelled as loud as he could as his face began to turn red, "We will build our armies and defeat our enemies!"

The entire auditorium erupted with a thunderous ovation as the people began to stand and clap uncontrollably. Adolf Hitler realized as he stared into the audience that when he spoke, he commanded authority. He looked over at Hermann, who was also clapping. He then turned his head to his right. He then glanced over at the party secretary Rudolf Hess, who acknowledged his response. He too was very jubilant. Rudolf had stood up, along with the other party members. They were giving Adolf the Nazi salute. The people started to shout, "Heil Hitler!" On this day Adolf Hitler had seen his destiny.

"Wilhelm, we must have a talk, young man," said his mother. The year was 1933. Wilhelm had gone home for the fall semester recess. They were sitting at the dinner table. "You have only been in medical school for two years."

"Yes, Mother, I know."

"Your father had worked very hard to give you this opportunity to make something out of your life!"

"Mother, I am twenty-one years old and capable of making my own decisions for myself."

"Yes, my son, I know you are a man now."

"Besides, Mother, I am still going to continue my medical training, except with the air force."

"Wilhelm, your father went to his grave wanting to give you the best education he could."

Wilhelm had started to remember how much he despised his father, the names that he would call him, and then there were the beatings. "Mother, with the Führer now being the chancellor of Germany and me being a member of the National Socialist Party, my service to the Führer and our country is very important to me."

"Yes, Wilhelm, I know. Adolf Hitler has done miraculous things for our people! But, son, I just cannot help but wonder what all of this means and what the future holds for our beloved Germany."

The automobiles were approaching the entrance to the Gildendolph Mansion. When they had arrived, the young German soldiers would snap to attention. They would open the doors to allow the guests out of their vehicles. The officers would step out accompanied by their lovely ladies, then the soldiers would raise their right arms and shout, "Heil Hitler!" It was an early summer night in 1934, a pleasant evening, and you could see all the stars in the heavens. The National Socialist Party (Nazi) was celebrating their annual banquet dinner. Some of the party's most elite members were arriving, including the Führer. It was around 9:15 p.m. when a black Mercedes pulled up to the entrance. "Heil Hitler!" the soldiers shouted when the car door, began to open. Stepping out of the vehicle, the cameras began to flash, the Nazi party photographers were taking pictures of the patrons arriving, standing tall and smiling as he got out of his Mercedes. Reich Marshal Hermann Goering. He then glanced at the direction of the photographers; he enjoyed the attention. He was followed by some of his junior officers. Among them was Lieutenant Wilhelm Strausvon.

The symphony orchestra band had begun to play. The melody of their music filled the auditorium. The guests were dancing. The caterers were delivering appetizers in the midst of the people. The smell of cigar smoke had filled the hall; the sound of laughter was heard. Suddenly, the band stopped playing, and the people stop talking; there was a complete silence in the place. "Heil Hitler!" the people began to shout. They all simultaneously extended there right arms. Adolf Hitler had arrived at the banquet. The Führer lazily raised his arm as it was his custom to do. Members of the party stood at attention while Adolf started to make his way to his table. When he was walking, he smiled at guests and stopped to shake hands with some of his generals and their wives.

The band continued to play, and people started to mingle again. There was laughter heard once again throughout the mansion. "Wilhelm," Hermann said.

Wilhelm was walking by. He was carrying two glasses of wine in his hands. "Yes, Reich Marshal Goering."

"Please, Wilhelm, call me Hermann. I want you to stop by my office tomorrow at 2:00 p.m."

"Okay, Hermann," replied Wilhelm.

Hermann was about to leave the banquet. He was quite drunk. He didn't want to make a fool of himself because he knew the Führer didn't tolerate drunkenness. He shook hands with some of the guests as he was leaving.

"I think the Reich Marshal has had too much to drink!"

"Bite your tongue, Karl," Wilhelm said.

Captain Karl Dietrich was twenty-four years old. He was six feet tall and a husky man. He was the brother of SS Reich General Sepp Dietrich. "Don't look now, but the girls are coming," Karl said. Wilhelm placed the wineglasses on the table. He then grabbed the hand of his fiancée. She had approached him as he was walking to their table. Marlene Weizmann was the younger sister of Gilda Dietrich, who was the wife of Karl. Marlene was a very attractive woman. She was five feet two and had blond hair and blue eyes.

Karl grabbed the hand of his beautiful wife, then the four of them made their way to the dance floor. The lights started to dim. The band was playing a song for couples to dance to. Wilhelm put his arm around Marlene's waist, and the two started to dance while they stared into each other's eyes; the couple was very much in love.

"Earlier, I saw you talking to the Reich Marshal. What did he want?"

Wilhelm pulled her closer to himself. "I have a 2:00 p.m. appointment at the Reichstag," Wilhelm whispered in her ear.

"Wilhelm dear, you must protest if you are going to be reassigned to another district."

"Don't worry, darling, I don't believe that's what the Reich Marshal has in store for me."

HE WAS ABOUT TO BETRAY HIS OATH

The couple continued to dance. Wilhelm looked over at Karl and Gilda. He thought to himself how fortunate he was to have a family. "Wilhelm," Marlene whispered, "I do not want us to be separated while I am pregnant." The two looked into each other's eyes, and they kissed.

The year was 1936. The Winter Olympic Games were being held in Berlin. The German capital of the third Reich was decked out in all its glory and splendor. Everywhere you looked, the Nazi flag with the symbol of the swastika hung on every building. The German people were proud to be hosting the games. The regime wanted to show the people of the world that Germany would no longer be a second-class nation. This was Adolf Hitler's moment to shine. The Führer wanted the rest of the world to take notice that Germany was alive and prosperous. The Berlin Olympic Stadium was filled to capacity. The people were proudly waving their flags and singing party hymns.

The German chancellor had arrived. The people were singing and chanting. "Heil Hitler! Heil Hitler!" echoed throughout the stadium. Adolf was escorted to his seat by Major Wilhelm Strausvon. The Führer gave his customary salute as he made his way to his luxury box seat. He then shook hands with Hermann when the two men greeted each other.

It started to snow. Then Deputy Secretary Rudolf Hess noticed the Führer had water dripping from his forehead. "My Führer," he said as he was handing him a handkerchief. Rudolf had started to explain to the Führer the schedule for the day's events while the Führer wiped his brow.

Reich Marshal Goering stood up. He gave the signal to let the Olympic Games begin. Suddenly the cages opened up from around the entire stadium. Six thousand doves were released into the air. The stadium was filled with the doves, then the people started to shout, "Heil Hitler!" A few moments later Adolf stood up; he returned the people's salute. But this time he stood with his right arm fully extended. After a few more moments, Adolf sat down.

The nations that were to participate in the Olympic Games began to march their athletes by the Nazi viewing stand. The French athletic team was to walk past the Nazi members next. When they approached the viewing stand, they turned toward the Führer, and they gave the Hitler salute. Adolf was having a conversation with Hermann when he was interrupted. "Look, my Führer, they're saluting you," Wilhelm said. He was sitting directly behind the Führer. Adolf heard the major. He looked up. Suddenly there was a smile on the German chancellor's face. He leaned to his right. Adolf said to Hermann, "They will be the easiest to conquer." Both men started to laugh uncontrollably while they stood to return their salute.

The javelin event had just finished when Rudolf began to explain the next event. He told the Führer that the track event was next. Suddenly there was the sound of a whistle, then the referee raised the starting gun. The sound of the starting gun went off—*bang!* Then all the runners that were lined up started to run.

The Americans were being represented by a black athlete, named Jesse Owens. It was the 200-meter race, and young Jesse was in full stride. He had run past all the other runners when he approached the finish line. Suddenly, the stadium got real quiet. The cheers turned into boos when Jesse Owens crossed the finish line; he had won the gold medal.

Adolf had watched the American team run to congratulate him. Hitler's face was filled with rage, then he started to yell at Deputy Secretary Hess, "We lost the race to a black man. I want answers. You have Dr. Strausvon handle this!"

"Right away, my Führer," Rudolf said. Adolf and Hermann got up. They both started to leave the stadium followed by some senior officers.

Wilhelm had heard what the Führer had said to Rudolf. He quickly made his way to where he was. Wilhelm sat down next to the deputy secretary. "Dr. Strausvon, I want you to make sure that the German track runner never runs again!"

"Yes, my deputy secretary," Wilhelm said. Major Wilhelm Strausvon stood up to leave. He glanced down at the German track team. With a smile on his face, Dr. Strausvon left the balcony area.

CHAPTER 2

A Call to Duty

The year was 1980. Most Americans were upset with the Carter administration's domestic and foreign policies. He was twenty years old when he had heard a campaign speech by presidential candidate Ronald Reagan. Mr. Reagan was explaining what was wrong with the country. Mr. Reagan said, "I am prepared to fix our economy, our military. America must lead the world against the evil of communism and terrorism!"

After hearing those words, he had said to himself, "I would love to serve under the administration of a charismatic leader, someone like Ronald Reagan."

Ronald Wilson Reagan was elected that fall. He became the fortieth president of the United States of America. So he had decided to enlist in the United States Navy in December of that year. He found himself headed to Great Lakes Naval Academy, in the state of Illinois.

The bus drove up to the front gate. He could see a military officer when he looked out of the bus window. The officer was approaching the bus, then the bus driver opened the door. The bus driver handed the officer some papers. A few moments later the gate started to retract. The bus started to drive forward. It was delivering the naval recruits to their destination. He had noticed sailors marching in the distance.

The blue bus pulled up to the barracks. It was a cold day. The sky was clear, and you could feel the wind blowing from Lake Michigan. "All right, ladies," the voice yelled. The bus doors started to open. The drill instructor was screaming at the top of his voice. "You maggots get off of my bus. Move it! Move it! I want your toes on the white line. For the next sixteen weeks your asses belong to me."

All he kept thinking was how cold it was standing in formation. The temperature had to be at least ten degrees. "I am Chief Petty Officer Davies," screamed the instructor. "When I ask you a question, you yell, 'Yes, sir, Chief!' Do you maggots understand?" The company of recruits started to yell, "Yes, sir, Chief!" Chief Petty Officer Davies was a huge man. He stood six feet three. He weighed at least 240 pounds. The chief had a voice that made you shake in your boots when he yelled.

The recruits were issued clothes and sleeping gear, then they all got their haircuts. None of the men recognized one another. They were all bald. They then marched back to their barracks. When the recruits entered through the door, they had encountered another drill instructor. Chief Davies screamed at them to find their beds by name, then to stand on the white line painted on the barracks floor, in front of their bunks. He then yelled, "You maggots have two minutes, understood?"

"Yes, sir, Chief," the company yelled.

He found his bunk and put his gear on the bed. He was assigned the top bunk. "I don't have all day," Chief Davies yelled. The recruits were standing on the white line that was painted down both sides of their barracks.

"My name is Chief Petty Officer Jeffries," the other drill instructor said while he walked down the middle of the barracks. "I am your company commander, your company number is 061. Remember it," Chief Jeffries said. Chief Jeffries was an older man. He was not as intimidating as Chief Davies. Chief Jeffries seemed to talk to them instead of yelling.

"You ladies can get acquainted with one another. There will be no chow tonight. Breakfast is at 0530, that's five thirty a.m. for you maggots who can't tell time," Chief Davies yelled.

"Dismissed," Chief Jeffries said.

He turned around looked at his new home for the next sixteen weeks. "What in the world have I gotten myself into?" He then looked at his shipmate, and he stared back at him, then they both had realized that this was going to be an experience that they would never forget.

"By the way, I should introduce myself, even though our names are on our lockers. I am Thomas Allen."

"Hello, Thomas. I'm Brian Singer." Both men started to shake hands, then Tom climbed up on the top bunk.

"So where are you from, Brian?"

"I am from Greenfield, New Hampshire. What about you, Tom? Where are you from?"

"I am from Buxton, Maine."

"Well, what do you know, two New Englanders stuck in the same hellhole," Brain said. Suddenly, the lights went out.

The sky was getting cloudy. The stars had disappeared. It was a warm summer night, and the mosquitoes were starting to bite. "Sweetheart, put another log on the fire. It's starting to go out," Joanne said. Joanne Shirosky was Tom's beautiful fiancée. She had black hair and blue eyes. She had a luscious body. They were camping in the White Mountains with some friends when it started to rain. "Hurry, Tom, I'm getting wet," Joanne said. The rain was coming down very hard, so they both ran into their tent.

Tom grabbed a towel. He started to dry off her face. That's when he looked into those beautiful eyes. Tom had realized just how much he loved her. They started to kiss passionately when it had started to thunder. *Crash! Boom!* The sound the thunder made.

Crash! Boom! That was what Tom heard when he began to wake up to the sound of aluminum garbage cans being tossed down the middle of the barracks aisle. "It's only a dream," he said to himself.

When Tom had realized that he was not camping, he then heard that awful voice yell, "Get your asses out of those bunks. I want your toes on the white line. Understand!"

"Yes, sir, Chief!" the recruits yelled while Chief Davies was walking down the main aisle.

"I swear he's the devil," Brian said as they made their way to the white line. Brian Singer was a few months older than Tom. Brian stood at five feet ten. He had black hair and brown eyes. He weighed at about 180 pounds. Both men looked like they could be brothers. "I think he's the Antichrist," replied Tom.

"You ladies have seven minutes to shit, shower, and shave, make your racks, get your asses outside in formation, understand!"

"Yes, sir, Chief!"

"Move it," Chief Davies yelled.

Within a few weeks, the men had learned how to march and live together as a unit. Company 061 was the finest bunch of seaman recruits that had ever assembled at Great Lakes Naval Academy. Their company was the envy of the entire base.

Dear Joanne,

How have you been these last few months? I hope and pray that all is well with you, and how's your mom doing? I miss you dearly. I can't wait to see you again. It has been a while since I have had some time to write. Boot camp is winding down. It is hard to believe that spring is just around the corner. In my last letter I wrote to you, I had been complaining about all the marching that we did. We now spend more time in class learning the history of our great nation. As for Chief Davies, he does not call us ladies anymore! We are now seamen. I got to put on my dress blues yesterday for fitting. I am proud to be a sailor. The weather is starting to get better here. The temperature is now in the high forties! Graduation is in two weeks. Brian and I are both going to be stationed at the Charleston Naval Base, in South Carolina. We are also on the same ship, the USS

Wainwright, a guided missile cruiser. I can't believe the navy has put us together. I guess we will be friends for life.

Joanne, I know that our lives together will prosper and our love for each other will continue to grow. The navy will enable us to have a very bright future together. I love you always. Write back soon.

Love,
Thomas
PS, I love you!

The year was 1984. President Reagan was running for reelection. During the previous four years Mr. Reagan had delivered on what he had promised. During his first term, the economy had started to flourish. His administration was confronting the Soviet Union. America was no longer a country of pessimism but had turned into a nation of optimism. The USS *Wainwright* was docked at her home port.

They had just returned from a six-month deployment with their battle group and air craft carrier USS *Saratoga*. Tom's four-year enlistment was almost over, but Brian wanted him to continue his navy career.

"Tom, I really think you should reenlist with me."

"Brian, I told you, let's just enjoy our liberty. We can talk about this later."

It was summer, and it was very hot and humid. The two men had shore leave. They were on their way to Myrtle Beach.

"Hail that taxi. We need get to the motel," Tom said to Brian. Brian hailed the taxi. The two sailors were on their way to the beach. "I can't wait to get out of these dress whites. Put on some swimming shorts so we can find some hot babes to meet," Tom said. They both looked at each other, and they started to smile.

The smell of the salty air and the sound of the crashing waves were what they could smell and hear. When Brian and Thomas left their motel, they were walking to the beach. "This is the life," Brian said while the two men were setting up their beach chairs. "You are absolutely right, my friend," Tom said. The two men had put on sunscreen, and they were taking in the sun's rays.

"Don't look now, but here come two cutie-pies, and one of them looks like Joanne," Brian said. While the two women were approaching, that's when Tom noticed some seagulls. They were flying in the background. He started to drift away.

The lights were very dim. The couple next to them were both laughing and holding hands. A waitress was pouring wine into Joanne's glass. She then proceeded to fill Tom's glass. Then Tom looked up. He started to stare into her blue eyes. "Joanne, you are very quiet this evening. Is there something wrong?"

A tear had started to flow. "Tom, I have something to tell you." Joanne picked up her napkin. She started to wipe the tear from her face. "I am seeing someone else, and we are in love!"

"Tom, Tom, Tom, snap out of it," Brian yelled.

"I'm seeing someone else" were the words that Tom heard her say to him. When the two women had walked by, Tom turned his head to watch them. That's when Tom realized that he needed to move on. "Brian, my friend, it's time that I forget about Joanne."

"Now you're talking, Tom. Let's go party tonight so we can meet some real women!"

CHAPTER 3

The Nursing Home

The year was 1988. The day was Monday, 10:00 a.m. He was headed to a job interview. It was a beautiful summer day. The sun was shining through the puffy white clouds. He had approached the entrance door and gathered his composure.

When he entered into the nursing home, he had noticed a nurse at the front desk who made eye contact with him. "May I help you?" she asked.

"Yes, you may. My name is Timothy Ferraro. I have a job interview with the housekeeping supervisor, Mr. Harry Jones." The nurse told Timothy to have a seat and that she would page Harry. Timothy went to sit down in the waiting lounge. While he was walking away, he could not help but feel an attraction to this nurse. Timothy had noticed when he glanced up from the magazine he was reading that she could not keep her eyes off him.

"Mr. Ferraro," a voice said. Timothy had looked up from reading the magazine. It was Mr. Jones. He had asked Timothy to follow him to his office. Harry was an older man in his fifties. He was six feet tall. He had grayish-black hair, and he wore glasses. While they walked, Timothy noticed that Harry started to whistle. This was a trademark that he could use to save himself many a times.

Timothy had his interview, and Harry wanted him to start the following Monday. Harry left the maintenance office to get some forms that Timothy needed to consent to. Upon his ability to start, he needed to have a physical and drug screening. Suddenly, Timmy heard someone entering the office. "Have you seen Harry?" the man asked.

"Yes, I have. He went to the personnel office."

"My name is Juan!"

"I'm Timmy." The two men shook hands, and they talked for a few minutes.

Timmy left the nursing home. When he was exiting the parking lot, he had to stop at the stop sign because of traffic. Timmy had looked through his driver's side mirror, and he saw the name Woodridge Nursing Home. Immediately, he heard those words again. "May I help you?" Those were the words that Timmy heard when he looked into her hazel eyes, then he wondered who the beautiful woman was.

It was Timmy's first day on the job. He worked with Juan for an hour on the third floor. Then he went to work on his floor. Timmy was sweeping the second-floor corridor when he walked by a room. He then glanced inside the room. Timmy saw a name on the door. It said Richard Rittenberg. Mr. Rittenberg was hooked up to a feeding tube. Timmy walked through the door. He heard a voice say, "Can I help you?"

There she stood near the door, long black hair, hazel eyes, and a beautiful smile. Her name tag said Donna Murphy. He started to speak to her, when he noticed the diamond ring on her finger. "Hello, I'm Timothy."

"I know who you are, and you still have not answered my question."

"I was just sweeping. I noticed this patient in this condition, and I was just wondering, what had happened to him?"

"Well, you just stay away from Mr. Rittenberg, Timothy," she said.

"Please, you can call me Timmy." Nurse Murphy and Timmy had started to walk down the corridor together. Donna had asked him how old he was. Timmy told her that he was twenty-eight. "How old are you Donna?"

"Timmy, hasn't anyone ever told you, never ask a woman her age!"

Timmy stopped walking. He stood there with a puzzled look on his face while he stared at Donna as she walked away. He started to wonder again to himself, "Who is this gorgeous woman?"

Timmy finished up his first day of work at the nursing home. He spoke with Harry before he had left. Harry had told him that he did very well for his first day. Timmy thanked him for his compliment. He then clocked out his time card, and he left the nursing home for the evening.

"There has been another gang-related shooting this afternoon, outside Fenway Park, following the Red Sox loss to the New York Yankees," the news reporter said.

"Good, let those kids kill each other so we don't have to pay for their prison terms!" Jonathan said. Jonathan Loveday was a tall man. He stood at six feet two. He weighed 230 pounds. Jonathan was an intimidating man.

It was August, and John was watching the local news. "John, dinner is ready," his fiancée yelled.

"It will be another hot day in New England. Tomorrow's temperature highs will be in the low nineties," the weatherman said.

"John, shut that television off. It's time to eat."

The telephone started ringing, and John reached for it.

"Hello, John. This is Laura." Laura Meagher was an attractive woman. She had brown hair and blue eyes. She was a very petite-looking woman. "Is Donna home?" she asked.

"Yes, she is, Laura, but we are getting ready to eat!"

Laura went on to explain to John to have Donna call her after they had finished dinner.

Donna asked John to pass the salt. They were discussing their day. "Honey, don't forget that I have a doctor's appointment tomorrow. I'll be late getting home."

"I haven't forgotten," John replied. He then began to chew on his steak.

Donna was driving to her doctor's appointment when the traffic became congested at an upcoming intersection. "That's just great, I'm stuck in all this traffic," she said. Donna blew her horn several times. She had decided to turn on her radio.

"It's Tuesday afternoon, and it's hot," the disc jockey said.

"No kidding!" Donna mumbled.

"Its 3:00 p.m. and currently ninety-two degrees. You're listening to 94.7 WHJI Providence. We are here to make your ride home a cool one. Here is a song from Steve Perry and his band Journey."

The music to the song started to play, then Donna screamed, "Yes, I love this song!" She then turned the volume up. She began to sing the lyrics. "Just a small town girl, living in a lonely world, he took the midnight train going anywhere. Just a city boy, born and raised in south Detroit, he took the midnight train going anywhere. A singer in a smoky room, the smell of wine and cheap perfume, for a smile they can share the night, it goes on and on and on and on!"

The traffic light changed to green, and Donna moved along with the flow of traffic. Another light just turned red again. While Donna was listening to the song, she began to ponder about her future. She had glanced at her belly, then the light changed to green. She gave her car a boost of acceleration and drove through the intersection.

It was your typical pediatrician's office. When you walked into the facility, you saw multiple colored children's chairs. There was Sesame Street wallpaper covering the walls. There was a toy box in the middle of the room. Donna was watching a group of four- and five-year-old boys playing. "Is this your first child?" the woman asked. She was sitting next to Donna.

"Yes," replied Donna. The boys were really having a good time playing. They were chasing each other and laughing as they ran. Donna and the woman continued to have a conversation. She had told Donna that the child wearing the blue overalls was hers. "He's cute," Donna said. The little boy ran over to his mother because he had a cold and he wanted her to wipe his nose.

"Laurie Briggs," the nurse yelled from her desk. "That's me," said the woman who was talking with Donna. She wished Donna good luck. She then yelled for her son to follow her while she was leaving the waiting room. Donna was browsing through a magazine when she heard the nurse call her name.

"Stand still," said the nurse. She was sliding the weight bar across the scale. The nurse wrote down Donna's height, weight, and vital signs. "Dr. Ramirez will be in shortly to see you, Ms. Murphy."

Donna had seen her doctor, so she decided to schedule another doctor's appointment. She was leaving the building when she began to smile. Donna then put on her sunglasses.

The door opened, and the little bells on the back started to jingle. The smell of coffee filled the room. Donna looked around and spotted Laura sitting in a booth at the back of the doughnut shop. "How long have you been waiting?" Donna asked.

"I got here about ten minutes ago," replied Laura. A waitress approached the women, and she asked them if they were ready to order. They both ordered coffee, light with two sugars.

"So how did your doctor's visit go?" asked Laura.

"It went well. The doctor told me that I was about twelve weeks."

"Have you told John yet?"

"No, Laura, I am afraid of what he will say!"

"Donna, he knows that you went to the doctor today."

"Laura, he thinks that I went in for a routine checkup."

Laura went on to tell Donna that soon she would be showing, and eventually, John would find out. She told her that it would be better to tell him now rather than later. Suddenly, there was a screeching sound and a loud bang. A few seconds later the door opened up in the little breakfast diner.

Does anyone here own a new blue Chevy IROC?" the man asked.

Donna stood up and said, "I do!"

"Lady, I think someone has hit your car and sped off."

Laura and Donna rushed outside the front door, where she had discovered that her driver's side front end was totally smashed. "That's just great. This is all I need. John is going to kill me, he loves this car!"

"Code yellow, room 222," the announcement came over the intercom. Timmy was washing the floor near Mr. Rittenberg's room. Suddenly there came a rush of nurses and Dr. Chapman. It was Ms. Carlton. She was having a serious medical problem. Margret Carlton was a sweet elderly lady. "I hope that she will be okay," Timmy mumbled. He was walking past her room as the door to her room began to close.

Later on that day, Timmy was sweeping the floor near the nurses' station when he observed the nurses and Dr. Chapman leaving Ms. Carlton's room. He then saw Laura and Donna walking toward there station desk.

"Hello, Timmy," Donna said. She was walking past him. The two nurses sat down at their station.

"Donna, have you heard any news about your car?" Laura asked.

"The insurance company said that it's not totaled," Donna replied.

"So, Donna, did you tell John yet?"

"No, Laura, I figured that he was upset enough about the accident yesterday."

"Donna, you know, you have to tell him that you're pregnant."

"Shhhh, here comes Timmy," Donna whispered. "Laura, can you give me a ride home today?"

"Donna I would love to, but Michelle Bettes asked me to work late tonight. Why can't John pick you up?"

"He left this morning for Miami. John won't be back till Saturday!"

"Did I hear someone say they needed a ride home today?" Timmy asked. Timmy had arrived at the nurses' station just as Donna whispered for Laura to be quiet.

Donna started to explain to Timmy that she had only known him for a few weeks, and she was about to decline his offer, but Laura convinced her to accept. Then Timmy said to Donna that during their ride, they would be able to talk and get to know each other better. Timmy told Donna that he would meet her at the employees' entrance after their shift ended.

"He is so cute," Donna said.

"I know," replied Laura. The two women started to giggle. They then watched Timmy while he was walking away. "Don't forget about that rock on your finger that Jonathan gave you," Laura said. Laura admired Donna's engagement ring.

Donna was leaving the building to meet Timmy when she saw his car pull up to the entrance door. She then noticed the car. She asked him what year it was. He said, "1985."

Donna then got into Timmy's car. That's when she had noticed that it was different from hers. She owned a Chevy Camaro IROC Z28. "Wow, your stereo swivels, and, Timmy, you have a digital speedometer," Donna said. Donna was fascinated with his car. She had asked Timmy what the brand name was.

"Chevy Camaro Berlinetta!" He then told her to buckle up because his car was just as fast as hers. Donna put on her seat belt, and together they sped off.

CHAPTER 4

World War II Part 1

It was winter, and the year was 1938. Europe was enjoying a peaceful winter. Many nations had sent their representatives to Germany to watch the German Military parade its mighty power. Hitler wanted to show the world that Germany was now a superpower. The Führer had stood with his arm extended. He was saluting his soldiers as they marched goose-stepping by. His tanks and artillery followed closely by.

Suddenly, there came a sound like thunder. The Luftwaffe was flying overhead; the German Air Force was impressive. A thousand planes were flying by. Reich Marshal Hermann Goering stood gazing up at his planes as they flew overhead. He looked over to Reich Minister Heinrich Himmler, who was the chief administrator of the SS, Germany's elite forces. They wore black uniforms. He said, "With my Luftwaffe and your troops, we shall rule the world." Both men began to laugh uncontrollably. SS General Sepp Dietrich also shared their enthusiasm.

All three men knew that in three months, on March 13, Adolf Hitler would decide that it was time to reunite the country of Austria with Germany, allowing Himmler's SS Panzer Divisions to enter the Austrian capital, Vienna. With the Luftwaffe providing air support, this act alone would set the stage for the complete takeover of the continent of Europe. Colonel Wilhelm Strausvon and Major Karl Dietrich were standing a few feet behind the Reich Marshal.

Wilhelm sat at his desk gazing out of his library window. He lived in a large Victorian-style house on a land that he owned. There was a small lake in the backyard. The window that he was viewing from was long and tall; it almost covered the entire wall of his study room. He was thinking about the war and about his past. Wilhelm put his pen down; he then stopped writing. He began to ponder on what his late mother had said to him. "Son, I just cannot help but wonder what all of this means and what the future holds for Germany!" He thought that by becoming a physician, he would be able to help save lives. Now his talents were being used to destroy human life. The Nazi regime was systematically annihilating a race of people.

Wilhelm had noticed a car pulling up in his driveway. He could see his wife and daughter exiting the vehicle. Kateland was running to the front door. He picked up his pen and continued to write in his journal.

Log entry 7/29/40

Today, I watched my beautiful wife and daughter arrive home safely from the marketplace. The war is not what I expected. Some of the SS officers have gone mad. They are rounding up Jews from the occupied territories and sending them to ghettos that are fenced in neighborhoods. The SS officers are drunk with hatred. These men shoot Jews randomly and laugh. It doesn't matter to them whether they are women or children.

Suddenly, there was a knock on his door. "Come in," Wilhelm said. The door slowly opened. "Happy birthday to you, happy birthday to you, happy birthday, dear Daddy. Happy birthday to you!" Those were the words that Wilhelm heard Marlene and Kateland sing when they came through the door. They were carrying a small chocolate cake, and there were five candles burning on the cake. "Daddy, blow out your candles," Kateland said. Wilhelm blew out the candles as the smoke drifted away. He had noticed how happy his daughter was. "Daddy, how old are you?"

"Well, Kateland, how old are you?" Wilhelm asked.

"This many," she said while she held up her hand to show her father. Wilhelm then asked her how many fingers she was showing. Kateland then looked at her fingers and she told him, "Five!"

"Well, you add five more hands, and that's about how old Daddy is." Marlene stood by observing her husband and daughter. She wished him a happy birthday, then she gave him a kiss. Marlene and Kateland then left the study room. She then closed door behind her. Wilhelm looked at his cake. He had thought about how fortunate he really was. He then thought about what Reich Marshal Goering had told him a few years ago. He said to Wilhelm that family wasn't important; only your loyalty to the Führer and the Third Reich. But Wilhelm thought to himself that Hermann was wrong, and the love for his wife and daughter had meant more to him than anything else in the world.

The telephone had started to ring. Wilhelm opened his eyes, and he looked at the clock. It said 2:15 a.m. "This had better be important!" he yelled.

"Hello, Colonel Strausvon, this is General Klaus Holzhausen."

"Yes, General, what can I do for you at this hour?" Wilhelm asked.

The general wanted Wilhelm to cut short his leave. He needed him to return to Alpha Base, which was located in the occupied territory inside of France. Wilhelm had assured the general that he was leaving at first light. Wilhelm hung up the phone, then he dialed headquarters.

"Heil Hitler, Corporal Hertz speaking."

"This is Colonel Strausvon!"

"Yes, Colonel, what can I do for you this morning?"

Wilhelm went on to explain to the corporal that he wanted his car to pick him up and to have his plane ready to leave immediately for Alpha Base. Marlene had been listening to what her husband was saying. She was pretending to be asleep while he was talking on the telephone. Wilhelm crawled over the bed to her side, and when he was climbing on the bed, she opened her eyes. He looked into her blue eyes. He then told her how much he loved her. Wilhelm then hugged and kissed her good-bye. She knew that it would be a long time before she would see him again.

Wilhelm arrived at the airport. He was accompanied by some of his staff. "Dr. Strausvon, I'm Captain Elbrerich. I will be flying you this morning out to Alpha Base!"

"Very well, Captain. Let's get going. Time is of essence."

"Yes, sir," Captain Elberich said. The plane taxied to the runway, then it started to take off. Colonel Strausvon looked out of his window when his plane flew over the Reichstag. Wilhelm noticed that the sun began to shine over the horizon. Wilhelm had thought to himself, "My beloved Berlin, what will become of you if the Allies start to bomb you!"

The air sirens had started to sound. The pilots began to scramble to their planes. The battle for Great Britain had begun. The Royal Air Force pilots knew that they only had a few minutes to get airborne. The Luftwaffe would cross the English Channel in less than ten minutes from their bases in occupied France.

Pilot, Major Nelson yelled to Captain Pierce! "What is it, Major? I can smell them sir," replied Nelson. "You boys know the drill. Stay in tight formation until we see those crosses on their planes," Captain Pierce said.

"There they are!" Lieutenant McBride yelled to the captain.

"Where?" asked Pierce.

"Two—no, three o'clock!" Lieutenant McBride yelled.

"Okay, boys, they're trying to hide in that cloud cover. Lieutenant McBride, you take Squad B. Follow me," said Major Nelson. "Captain Pierce, you take Squad D. You come in from the west."

"Let's go get them, boys," replied Pierce.

"Let's go, boys. We need to shoot down all their planes!" Lieutenant McBride yelled.

Squads A and B began to fly right into the German fighters. The German Messerschmitt planes started to roll left and right. They were trying to avoid the RAF Hawker Hurricanes and Supermarine Spitfires.

"Sullivan, pull up," Lieutenant McBride yelled. He had just watched his friend's plane burn and crash into the English Channel. Squads C and D had now entered into the fight.

"I got one, look at that baby burn," Captain Pierce yelled.

"Well done, boys," Major Nelson said. He began to praise his men. On this day the German Luftwaffe was no match for Briton's Royal Air Force. "God save the Queen!" Major Nelson yelled.

"Dr. Strausvon, we got more wounded coming in from the battle over Britain," Nurse Ingrid Kaufmann said. Ingrid was a gorgeous woman; she had long blond hair, green eyes, and a body a man would kill for. Ingrid was in her early thirties. She was assigned by the Reich Marshal to assist Wilhelm.

Dr. Strausvon yelled, "Code red," as his nurses and assistant doctors began to scramble. The wounded Luftwaffe pilots were landing; some of their fighter planes had been really shot up. Some pilots had severe burns and gunshot wounds. "Doctor, am I going to die?" asked the pilot. He was bleeding profusely from his left arm. "No, son, you'll be fine," Wilhelm said. "Nurse Kaufmann."

"Yes, Dr. Strausvon!"

"Take this brave pilot to the amputee ward. His arm needs to be amputated," Wilhelm whispered. The German Luftwaffe had bitten off more than they could chew. The British Royal Air Force was more of a potentiate adversary than the Germans had anticipated. Their casualty rate and losses of planes were enormous. The Führer was getting impatient, so he ordered Reich Marshal Goering to the Wolf's Den, a secret Nazi base in Bavaria at the southern part of Germany. There was about to be a change of plans for the Battle of Britain.

It was September 11, 1940. The battle for Britain was about to take on a different meaning. Hitler had ordered the Luftwaffe to bring the British people to their knees. He had ordered the destruction of the city of London. He told Hermann Goering to bring in the medium-range bombers.

The telephone rang. Wilhelm had to run out of the bathroom to answer it. It was Marlene. She had called him to inform him that she and Kateland were going to the Berlin theater tomorrow afternoon. She went on to explain that Karl and Gilda wanted to take them out for the day. She had told her sister that she was tired of being cooped up in the house. Wilhelm told her to have a good time and that he understood. He said that in a couple of weeks he would be taking leave again.

"Wilhelm, I love you," Marlene said. She then hung up the phone.

The air sirens started to sound. The RAF pilots started to scramble to their planes. "Okay, boys, you know the drill," Major Nelson said. This time the Luftwaffe fighter planes were escorting their bombers. They were cruising at thirty thousand feet. Major Nelson ordered Lieutenant McBride to take his squadron and to engage their heavy bombers. The rest of the squadrons would take on their fighters. "I think those bombers are headed to London!" Captain Pierce yelled.

The German Air Force had decided to bring the battle to the people of London. Hermann Goering had ordered the destruction of the British capital. The city was bombed, and the British prime minister Winston Churchill was furious. "We shall fight on the beaches. We shall fight in the Fields. We shall fight in the streets. However long it takes, we shall never surrender," he said.

Wilhelm looked out of his window. He could see the stars. It was a clear night, and there was a new moon. He pulled down the shade and lit some candles. Wilhelm then turned off the lights. Wilhelm was sitting on the bed watching the bathroom door, waiting for her to come out. The door opened, and she appeared. She was wearing a red lingerie. The scent of her perfume began to fill the bedroom. Wilhelm stood up when she started to move toward him.

His eyes began to follow her every movement. She was beautiful, he thought to himself.

"Oh, Wilhelm, I have waited all day for this moment to come." Wilhelm wrapped his arms around her waist, then both of them started to kiss. Her lips were as soft as satin. They kissed passionately. Wilhelm slowly removed her garment; it fell past her waist. Her breasts were white like snow; her skin was soft as cotton. Wilhelm picked her up. He then carried her to the bed, where they made love to each other. Afterward, they had fallen asleep.

The sun was shining brightly on Wilhelm's face. He was walking toward the screams. He could hear them getting louder the closer he got. "Help me, help me," screamed the voice. Wilhelm appeared on top of the hill. That's when he heard that deafening cry.

That's when Wilhelm saw her. She was wearing no clothes. There was man on top of her. "Quiet, you whore," he said, then he slapped her face, took out a knife, and stabbed her repeatedly. Until she stopped screaming. That's when Wilhelm slipped; he then fell. The man looked up. He saw Wilhelm watching him. Wilhelm turned around, and the boy started to run. "Come here, you little bastard. You can't outrun me, do you hear me, son?"

"No! No! No!"

"Wilhelm, wake up, wake up! You're having another bad dream."

Wilhelm woke up. There was sweat pouring down his face.

"Are you all right? It's your father again. You must learn to let your childhood go."

Wilhelm turned. He then looked at her blond hair, and then he looked into her green eyes. "Something terrible is going to happen, Ingrid."

"What do you mean?"

"I don't know, but I feel that there is going to be trouble."

The day was just like any ordinary day for the people living in the capital of the Third Reich. The streets were flowing with cars; people were moving in various directions. Some people had stopped to browse at some of the merchandise that was for sale in the stores' glass displays. The temperature that day was in the midfifties. The sky was partly cloudy. You could feel that fall was in the air and summer was winding down.

The air sirens began to sound. People stood looking at each other. They looked like they were wondering what was going on. The German government was not prepared for air attacks on its cities. Unlike the British, the Germans had not fully developed radar. The Royal Air Force was fighting back; they sent two squadrons of B-17 bombers. They were flying over Berlin. The Battle of Berlin had begun. The Luftwaffe had scrambled some fighters. By the time they were airborne, the B-17s had released their payloads.

Bombs had fallen. People were running and screaming as buildings were crumbling. Fires started burning simultaneously as the ground shook. A bomb landed in the parking lot next to the Berlin movie theater. The building shook violently, then it started to collapse. "Gilda, Gilda!" Karl yelled. He had tried to drag himself toward the light that was coming from a crack in the wall. His legs were pinned beneath a slab of concrete.

The air was full of smoke and soot. In the crowded space, it was hard to breath. You could hear people moaning and groaning. "Marlene, Kateland!" Karl yelled. There were sounds of the ceilings beginning to crumble around the tiny space where Karl was pinned. "I'm getting cold," Karl mumbled as he began to lose consciousness.

CHAPTER 5

The Agency Part 1

You could hear the sound of typewriters and telephones ringing throughout the office. It was a large room with various desks and tables. Thomas had decided that he was not going to reenlist in the navy. The year was 1985, and Thomas Allen had joined the Drug Enforcement Agency. He wanted to continue his oath by serving his country working for the Justice Department.

Thomas was sitting at his desk talking with his partner, Agent Lisa Crosby.

"Agents Crosby and Allen, in my office," Captain Donovan yelled. Captain Paul Donovan ran the Narcotic Investigative Unit of the agency. Paul was a short husky black fellow; he looked like he didn't need to eat any more doughnuts. But when the captain yelled, everyone in the unit could hear him.

Fighting between the Nicaraguan Army and the United States–supported rebels intensified in 1985 with the outcome uncertain. President Reagan's administration apparently was seeking the overthrow of the leftist regime. It stepped up its rhetoric against the Sandinista government. Behind the scenes, the Columbian drug cartel started to work with the Sandinista contras to export cocaine to the United States at a rate that was beginning to trouble the Reagan administration.

HE WAS ABOUT TO BETRAY HIS OATH

The year was 1988. Thomas was given an undercover assignment along with his partner, Agent Lisa Crosby. They were both in the captain's office. "Congratulations, Agent Allen, on your successful admittance," Captain Donovan said. "Lisa, it seems your observation of our subject was right on the money."

"Well, thank you, Captain Donovan," Lisa replied. Lisa had been working undercover for the past three months. She had established a relationship with the suspect, Donna Murphy. Her fiancé, Jonathan Loveday, had been under surveillance for the past four months.

"Agent Crosby, bring us up to speed on Operation Barracuda," Captain Donovan said.

"John and Donna have been in a relationship, according to her, for the past two years. She knows that John has inherited Three Eleven Restaurant in Miami, a small family steak house business owned by his deceased father."

"Lisa, how has Jonathan been able to keep his illegal activities from her? Is she even aware of what he has been doing these past few months?" Agent Steven Enos said.

"I don't know," replied Lisa.

"I think that's were Agent Allen comes in. He has been able to infiltrate the suspect's residence by planting listening devices," Lieutenant Donald Stickles said.

Agent Crosby was convinced that Agent Allen would have the best chance to get evidence on suspects Jonathan Loveday and Donna Murphy. The agency had done exclusive background checks on each suspect, but neither one had had a record. Lisa went on to say that she agreed with Lieutenant Stickles that Thomas should continue to develop a relationship with Donna. She felt that Donna's attraction to Agent Allen could lead them to solving their case.

Jonathan had boarded Pan American flight 397 to Miami, Florida. He was followed closely by Agent Kevin Crainey. The airplane started to taxi to the runway. It was scheduled to leave Logan International Airport at 11:00 a.m. Flight 397 took off after being delayed for forty-five minutes. The plane had climbed to cruising altitude when the captain suspended flight restrictions.

Agent Crainey had joined the DEA in 1983. He was formally a United States Navy SEAL. Kevin stood six feet four and weighed 235 pounds. He had a black belt in judo. Agent Kevin Crainey knew how to take care of himself. Agent Crainey and Agent Allen had a very close bond. They were good friends.

    Kevin was seated nine rows behind John. He was able to keep close surveillance on him. The flight attendant had pushed her meal cart next to Kevin. "Sir, would you like something to drink?"

    "Yes, ma'am, I'll have a Sprite!" Kevin watched her pour his soda. He was looking at her breasts and her name tag. It said Kathy.

    Agents Allen and Crosby had left the captain's office. They were sitting at their desks. They were finishing their paperwork for the night. Lisa had her desk directly in front of Tom's. It was the first time they could really speak to each other. Tom had looked up at the clock on the wall that was behind Lisa; it said 8:45 p.m. "So are you going to fill me in on exactly what happen this afternoon when you dropped her off?" Lisa said.

    "I was strapping in my T-roofs when Donna came out of the employees' entrance. She said, 'You have a nice car!'"

    "No, Tom, I don't want to hear about your ride. Tell me what happened when you took Donna to her house."

    Tom went on to explain to his partner what happened when he drove Donna home from work. He told Lisa that after they had pulled into her driveway, Donna invited him in for a drink. She lived in a beautiful large Victorian-style home. The front door had two large solid oak doors, with large brass handles. When you walked into the foyer, you could see huge paintings mounted on the walls. They were well preserved. Tom continued to enter the rest of her house. He was amazed at how beautiful her home was. Lisa continued to listen to what Tom was saying as she turned her head to look at the clock.

    "Their living room was enormous. She had a chandelier directly over an antique piano in the middle of the room. We made our way outside to the patio, that's when I noticed a decent-sized pond. In their backyard Donna made me a drink. We sat in her patio chairs, then a few minutes later, I gave her the excuse that I needed to use the bathroom. I then proceeded to plant my listening devices in the living room and bathroom."

"Now that's James Bond material," Lisa said with a chuckle.

"Lisa, does she have any relatives?"

"I don't think so, Tom. Our background records state that she is an only child. Her mother passed away when she was twenty! Donna is the lone beneficiary to her estate. By the way, Tom, I think you should know that she is pregnant."

It was 9:30 p.m. Tom wanted to go home. He needed to be in a little early tomorrow morning for work. Harry had a project for him and Juan to do. Tom said good night to Lisa. He then told her that he would see her at work. Tom left the precinct. Lisa was sitting at her desk finishing some paperwork when the telephone started to ring.

"Hello!"

"Lisa, it's Linda."

"What's up with my little sister?"

Linda had called her sister to inform her that she was having a birthday party for her daughter. Linda wanted to invite Lisa to her to niece's party.

The sun was shining through the crack of the window shade. He could feel the warmth of the glare on his face. Suddenly, the alarm clock sounded. "Wake up, you radio listeners," the announcer said. He was announcing that it was Thursday, and it was 6:30 a.m. He then went on to say, "This next song should get you motivated. It's by the Everly Brothers. Here's 'Wake Up Little Susie' right here on your classic oldies station, WKLX 100.7 Boston."

Tom jumped out of his bed. He headed straight for the bathroom. He then took a shower. Tom was looking in the mirror when he began to brush his teeth. He had noticed that his cat, Ozzy, was watching him. "I'm going to feed you before I leave!"

Tom left his house. He was driving to work. Tom noticed how muggy it was. "It's going to be a hot one today," Tom said.

Agent Christopher Gilmartin was responsible for surveillance of Jonathan Loveday during the night shift. John owned a house in a quiet middle-class neighborhood in Miami. Chris was parked about thirty yards down the street from his house. Two more agents we're posing as cable men repairing the cable wires. They were parked another twenty yards from Chris, on the opposite side of the street.

Agent Kevin Crainey had pulled up to relieve Agent Gilmartin. Kevin positioned his vehicle so he could continue surveillance. The DEA had tapped Mr. Loveday's phone, so at 8:00 a.m., when it started to ring, Kevin was listening. The man on the telephone wanted John to meet him at 2:00 p.m. on the pier dock at Watson Island. The Drug Enforcement Agency had set up further surveillance teams at the docks.

Timmy arrived at work. When he pulled into the parking lot, he realized that he had forgotten to feed his cat, Ozzy. "Good morning, Harry," Timmy said. Harry and Juan were waiting for Timmy to arrive. They went down to the activity room. Harry wanted them to refinish the floor.

It was breakfast time. Some of the residents were being escorted to the dining room. "Easy does it, Walter," Stacy said. Stacy was a nursing assistant. She was helping Mr. Benoit. He was pushing his walker. Walter Benoit was a large man. He was six feet five. He weighed over 280 pounds.

It was around 8:30 a.m. Juan and Timmy were waxing the floor when Laura came running to the activity room's entrance. "Timmy, I need to speak with you for a moment!"

"What's wrong, Laura?"

"It's Donna. She was helping Stacy pick up Mr. Benoit after he had fallen on the floor. She started to bleed and complained of stomach pains. Donna was then rushed to Cardinal Cushing Hospital."

CHAPTER 6

World War II Part 2

It was the fall of 1944. German cities were constantly being bombed by the Allied air forces. Reich Marshal Goering had ordered the eastern front division of the Luftwaffe to fifty miles outside of the industrial city of Dusseldorf. The Germans needed to protect most of their steel operating plants from Allied air attacks. Major General Wilhelm Strausvon had decided to name their base Kateland after his deceased daughter. Wilhelm was now in charge of all the Luftwaffe missions in defending the German city of Dusseldorf. The city was constantly being bombed by British and American air forces, day and night.

The Axis Powers were losing ground on all fronts of the war. Goering was under strict orders from the Führer to defend the city. D-day had come in June. The American divisions, headed by General George S. Patton, were closing in on the Rhine River. Wilhelm had confiscated a large mansion that was previously owned by a wealthy Jewish businessman. He had been sent to the concentration camp of Dachau. Wilhelm was in his study. He had been writing in his journal. He needed to be careful what he was writing so that no one would see, because he would be considered a traitor to the Third Reich.

Wilhelm was very upset with the outcome of the war. With the death of his wife and daughter, it had left him distraught. He blamed Hitler for the devastation of his country. Wilhelm watched Germany become a superpower and then become a nation that was losing on both fronts of the war. He knew that the end was inevitable and that the war was lost. So did the upper brass, but they were not saying anything. They knew that the Führer had lost his mind. All the phantom divisions that he was talking about, they did not exist.

Wilhelm knew that he needed to start covering his tracks he had noticed since he became a brigadier general during the early summer of 1942. Wilhelm understood that the Allies were not bombing the city of Nuremberg. So he sent Ingrid there, along with a young doctor, Lieutenant Hans Schmidt. Hans had reminded Wilhelm of himself when he was his age. They were ordered to set up a small clinic to render services to civilians and military personnel in need of medical assistance. Dr. Schmidt had family near the city of Nuremberg. His father was friends with the mayor. Wilhelm rented a house in the country for him and Ingrid to live. He thought by establishing ties in the community, this would help him and Ingrid to pass as civilians.

It was early March in 1945. The Third Reich was crumbling. The Allies had gained complete control of the skies over Germany. The Luftwaffe was decimated. Hitler spent all of his time in his underground bunker next to the Reichstag. The capital of the Third Reich lay in ruins. Hermann Goering was trying to salvage some of his personal artifacts. "Major, I want all my art moved to my underground bunker."

"Yes, my Reich Marshal," replied the major.

The German soldiers were taking some of Europe's finest art that was stolen by Hermann Goering during the Nazi looting that took place after a country was occupied.

"Major, I want this brass coffin-sized trunk placed on that truck parked next to my car. I want that truck guarded, and no one is to have access to that truck, understood?"

"Yes, sir, Reich Marshal." The major did exactly what was ordered of him. Hermann got into his car. He ordered his driver too drive to SS headquarters. The truck followed closely.

HE WAS ABOUT TO BETRAY HIS OATH

SS Reich Minister Heinrich Himmler had moved his staff outside the capital to the city of Hannover. He wanted to escape the Allied bombing of Berlin. Hermann's vehicle pulled up to the gate, where a guard proceeded to check his papers. When he realized who it was, he snapped to attention. He gave Hermann the Nazi salute, then he raised the gates arm they proceeded to the front entrance to the building.

Hermann stepped out of his car. The German soldiers snapped to attention. They shouted, "Heil Hitler!" when the Reich Marshal walked by. Hermann climbed up a flight of stairs. He went inside the building. Hermann was walking to Heinrich's office when he noticed pictures of a young jubilant Hitler all over the walls. He began to think to himself that he would not be in this mess that he found himself in if he had been in charge. Hermann entered Heinrich's office. Both men shook hands.

"What can I do for you?" Heinrich asked.

"The war is lost. We need to prepare for the inevitable," Hermann said. Hermann went on to explain to his friend that he had a way of saving their skins. He told Heinrich that he had a coffin-sized trunk full of gold coins and bars. Hermann then said that he wanted to hide the gold at the bottom of a lake, just outside the city. He then told Heinrich that General Strausvon had set up a clinic in Nuremberg.

"There is a safe house just outside of that city, and we could lie low for a while. Dr. Strausvon would help us to alter our appearance. Then, my friend, we could retrieve the gold and make our way to South America."

Heinrich liked the plan, so he asked Hermann, "What do you need from me?"

"I need one of your most trusted officers and a dozen of your elite troops loyal to the Führer," Hermann said. Heinrich Himmler had summoned a captain. He then told the captain to do whatever the Reich Marshal ordered him to do. Both men had left Heinrich's office. They went outside. "Major," Hermann said.

"Yes, my Reich Marshal."

Hermann informed his trusted officer that he wanted him to give him one of his most loyal sergeants and six of his soldiers. They were to accompany him and the Waffen SS soldiers. Hermann left the SS compound. They were driving to the lake. The truck carrying the gold was following right behind his vehicle, and following them in the distance was the Waffen SS. "Driver, turn on the radio. I want to hear if we are still broadcasting on our airwaves," Hermann said. The driver turned on the radio, but all you could hear was static. He started to turn the knob, then a station had come in.

"This is the BBC. If there any German soldiers who are listening, we ask you to surrender. The war is over for you. Your Führer is hiding like a coward. There is no reason for you to die."

"That's enough. Turn that damn radio off," Hermann said. The driver turned off the radio. Hermann started to laugh uncontrollably. He had known that the announcer on the radio was right; the Führer was a coward. The convoy of trucks drove through the countryside. They were on their way to the lake. The sky was getting cloudy. It looked like it was soon going to snow.

The convoy of trucks had passed the water tower. Hermann ordered his driver to pull over. He told him to keep the car running. It was a cold day, and Hermann wanted to return to a warm vehicle. Hermann Goering got out of his Mercedes. He climbed into the truck that was carrying the gold. "Sergeant, turn right and follow that road to the lake," Hermann said. The sergeant did what he was told. The truck had reached the end of the road. The lake was right in the foreground. Hermann climbed out of the truck. He then ordered his men to take the coffin-sized trunk one hundred yards out on the lake, dig a hole in the ice, and sink it. He then climbed back into the truck. Hermann watched his men carry out his orders. The soldiers carried the black chest to the ice, then they started to push it on the ice. Hermann took out his revolver from its holster. He then opened up the bullet chamber. He then checked to make sure he had all six bullets loaded in his weapon.

The truck left the lake and drove back onto the main road. Hermann climbed out. He got back into his car. They started to drive back to the SS compound when they had approached a roadblock. The Waffen SS captain allowed the Reich Marshal's Mercedes to proceed through. But they stopped the truck that was carrying the

HE WAS ABOUT TO BETRAY HIS OATH

Luftwaffe soldiers. The Waffen SS captain ordered his men to open fire. They fired their machine guns into the truck. The captain went to the back of the truck. He then lifted the canvas. There was blood everywhere. All the Luftwaffe soldiers were dead.

Suddenly, an American P-51 Mustang fighter plane flew overhead and buzzed the soldiers. They quickly took cover in the trees next to the side of the road. The plane circled back around for another pass. The pilot fired his cannons, making golf-ball-size bullet holes into the parked trucks. The pilot then began to pull up for another pass.

"Fire your weapons on his next pass!" the captain yelled. The plane came in again for another pass and fired its guns; it then started to pull up. Then the Waffen SS soldiers fired their machine guns. The fighter plane started to send out black smoke from its tail section. You could hear the engine start to sputter as it sent out flames and smoke.

"Driver, step on it," Hermann said. The vehicle started to speed up. Hermann knew that time was getting short. He needed to take care of some unfinished business at the compound. His car pulled up to the entrance. As he climbed out, the SS soldiers stood at attention. They shouted, "Heil Hitler!" Hermann climbed the flight of stairs. He then walked to Heinrich's office.

"How did it go?" asked Heinrich. Hermann had just walked into his office. "We are all set. The gold is in a safe place, and my soldiers are all dead!" Hermann walked over to the bar. He began to pour himself a shot of whisky. Heinrich was sitting at his desk. While Hermann poured his whisky, he looked at Heinrich.

"A toast," Hermann proposed. He was carrying a glass for the Reich Minister. He walked to the side of Heinrich's desk. He put the shot glass down on the desk, but when Heinrich reached for it, Hermann pulled out his revolver. He then shot Heinrich in his temple. Suddenly, Hermann heard the door to the office start to open. Hermann quickly put his gun in Heinrich's hand, and he placed it on the desk. The soldier had entered the room. "Corporal," Hermann said.

"Yes, Reich Marshal."

"Himmler has just committed suicide. What do you see?"

"I see that the Reich Minister has committed suicide, Reich Marshal."

"Very well, Corporal. Go get your superior and bring him here to me."

"Heil Hitler!" said the corporal. He then turned and ran out of the office.

Hermann then picked up his glass of whisky. He had placed it next to Heinrich's desk on a table stand, then he drank it. Hermann walked back over to the bar. He started to pour himself another shot. He walked back to the desk where Heinrich lay. Hermann looked at his lifeless body, then he looked out the window. The window was right next to the desk. It was snowing.

"I despise the winter," he said. Hermann then turned. He then looked at Heinrich. Hermann then drank the glass of whisky. He said, "Nobody is going to share my millions of dollars of gold, not even you, my friend."

In the month of May 1945, the German Army had surrendered. Adolf Hitler had committed suicide the previous month. Wilhelm had relocated to his medical clinic in Nuremberg. It seemed that his plan was working. Wilhelm was passing himself off as a civilian doctor. General Dwight D. Eisenhower was the supreme Allied commander of the occupation of Germany. The Nazi regime had committed terrible atrocities against humanity. They had constructed concentration camps in some of the occupied territory, with the intent of annihilating the Jewish race. The American, British, and Russian governments wanted to seek justice for the Nazi's systematic genocide and for the war crimes that Germany had committed in its conquest of Europe, Asia, and North Africa.

The Nazi war crimes tribunal of Nuremberg had begun. General Eisenhower, being from a German descent, wanted an American German officer to be in charge of the prison at Nuremberg. He chose Colonel Bonheoffer to lead the operation. The colonel quickly set up his command at the newly constructed prison that the American Army had built.

HE WAS ABOUT TO BETRAY HIS OATH

The Americans had received a tip that some senior Nazi officials were hiding in an underground bunker in the basement at a safe house just outside the city. The army had acted on this tip and raided the shelter. They had soon discovered that they had captured the number two ranking Nazi. Reich Marshal Hermann Goering was now a prisoner of the Allied occupation.

Wilhelm Strausvon was now thirty-three years old. He was quietly celebrating his birthday. The entire time he kept thinking when the Americans were going to find out that he was a former Nazi. Wilhelm had been spending long days at the clinic to pass the time. Ingrid came into his office. She wanted to cheer him up.

"Wilhelm, stop worrying. You are a genius. You have covered your trail. The Americans do not have a clue about your past." Wilhelm looked into her green eyes. He then got up from his desk and walked over to the window. Wilhelm was staring out the window. He was watching a young couple holding hands; they were walking by on the sidewalk.

"Wilhelm, am I not attractive to you anymore, and why won't you marry me? Do you still love me?" Wilhelm turned around from looking out of the window. He then smiled at Ingrid. "Of course I love you, darling!" He then kissed her on the lips. Then Dr. Strausvon went to attend to some patients.

It was a beautiful summer day. The rebuilding of Germany was under way. The Allies were shipping food and medical supplies to the medical facilities across the nation. The American Army had delivered medical supplies to the clinic before, but this time was different. They entered the premises with such authority that Wilhelm thought he was being arrested.

"Dr. Wilhelm Strausvon," the sergeant said.

"Yes," replied Wilhelm.

"Colonel Bonheoffer wants to see you at the prison compound."

"Am I under arrest?" asked Wilhelm.

"No," the sergeant said.

Wilhelm then left the clinic. He then climbed into the front seat of the military jeep. While they were traveling to the compound, he had begun to ponder where he had heard the name Bonheoffer before. The jeep traveled at a high speed Wilhelm looked at the backseat. He noticed that the military police officer was smiling. He started to think to himself that this situation didn't look promising.

The army jeep pulled up to the gate. The driver showed some identification. He then proceeded to drive to the administration building. Wilhelm got out of the jeep. He then followed the two soldiers into the building. When he entered through the entrance door, he noticed that American flags were hanging from the ceiling. Wilhelm had thought about the past when such buildings displayed the German swastika flags in buildings in his country. "Times have changed," he mumbled.

Wilhelm walked down a long hallway. There were people sitting at their desks typing. Telephones were ringing everywhere at the same time. The smell of cigarettes filled the room. Wilhelm had noticed that there were American women throughout the facility. They then reached the end of the corridor that led to a large office room; there was a bench next to a wall.

"Have a seat, Dr. Strausvon," the sergeant said. The other soldier stood guard over Wilhelm. The sergeant opened the office door next to the bench. He then went in. Wilhelm started to look around. He noticed the clock on the wall in front of him said 3:15 p.m. Below the clock hung two portraits. The one on the left was British prime minister Winston Churchill. On the right was the American president Harry S. Truman. Wilhelm was staring at the portraits when the office door opened.

"Dr. Strausvon, Colonel Bonheoffer will now see you," the sergeant said. Wilhelm walked into the office. When he had looked up, he couldn't believe his eyes. Both men started to smile. "It's really you," Wilhelm said.

"Yes, it is," replied the colonel. Both men shook hands and hugged each other.

"My ride over here, I kept thinking about your last name, how familiar it sounded. So how long has it been, Albert, since we've last seen each other?" Albert then dismissed the sergeant. The two men

HE WAS ABOUT TO BETRAY HIS OATH

began to reminisce about the time they were kids. "So you moved to the United States?" Wilhelm said.

"Yes, we settled in New York." Both men started to talk about the war and the devastation that faced the German people.

"So, Albert, what can I do for you?"

"I have a prisoner who needs medical treatment. He insists on only being treated by you."

"Who is he?" Wilhelm asked.

"Hermann Goering!"

Wilhelm had been drinking a glass of water when Albert had told him some semiclassified news. He then froze for a moment. He then choked on his water.

"Are you all right?"

"Yes, I am," replied Wilhelm. The two men then sat down. Albert went on to explain that Hermann had been complaining about a toothache that was causing him a severe headache.

"Sergeant," Colonel Bonheoffer yelled. Albert told the sergeant to escort Dr. Strausvon to see Mr. Goering. Wilhelm stood up. He then shook hands with his childhood friend Albert. The two men agreed to have dinner together later during the week.

Wilhelm arrived at the prison. It was a few hundred yards from the administration building. He was led into a small room. Wilhelm knew that the Americans were listening. Hermann was escorted to the room. He had chains on his hands and feet. Hermann looked at Wilhelm as he sat down. Wilhelm was totally shocked at what he saw. Here was the second most powerful man in Hitler's Third Reich looking so frail and pitiful. The Reich Marshal had lost a lot of weight, and he looked like he hadn't slept in days. Wilhelm did not want this fate to happen to him. He had thought about what Ingrid had said to him. "Wilhelm, stop worrying. You are a genius. You have covered your trail. The Americans do not have a clue about your past." Wilhelm was not about to let this despicable person ruin what he had worked for since the war ended.

He was remembering the banquet dinner when he was a young lieutenant when the Reich Marshal had said to him, "You can call me Hermann."

"Hermann, what can I do for you?" The two men were sitting opposite each other at a wooden table. Hermann bent over the table leaning toward Wilhelm. He then looked at the glass window to his left. There was a soldier watching his every move.

Hermann began to whisper to Wilhelm, "I need your help, my friend." Wilhelm had a look of concern on his face. He began to think to himself, what if he did not help Hermann?

"What can I do?" Wilhelm asked. Hermann went on to explain that he was going to be tried for crimes against humanity and that he wanted Wilhelm to help him commit suicide. He told Wilhelm that if he helped him, he would give him the location to where there was a brass chest the size of a coffin, full of gold bars and coins worth millions of dollars.

Wilhelm bent a little closer to Hermann. He then looked to his right at the guard through the window. Wilhelm then whispered, "This is what I will do for you." Wilhelm explained to Hermann that he would arrange for him to go the base clinic, where he would remove some of his molar teeth. Then he would make a set of false teeth. Inside one of the false tooth, there would be a cyanide capsule. "Hermann, all you would have to do is break open the tooth and bite the capsule. In a few seconds you will be dead."

"Very well, General Strausvon."

Wilhelm quickly corrected Hermann. "That's Dr. Strausvon," Wilhelm said. He then looked at the Reich Marshal, stood up from the chair he was sitting on, and he left. Wilhelm did what he had promised. The next day he provided Hermann Goering with a way out of his predicament.

Later in the week, Wilhelm met Colonel Bonhoeffer for dinner. The colonel had a proposition for Wilhelm. The two men had shook hands. They sat down at the table to eat. The waiter came over to their table. He then asked if the two men would like something to drink. The restaurant was a local pub that military personnel visited frequently. "I'll have a beer," Wilhelm said. "And you, Colonel?"

"I'll have gin and tonic!" The waiter wrote down their orders. He then left their table. Albert went on to explain to Wilhelm that there was a train leaving Saturday to a port in France. A ship was leaving next Friday for the United States. On that ship, there would be some German military personnel and scientists that his government wanted to bring to the United States. Albert opened up his brief case. He then pulled out some passports and credentials. Albert then gave them to Wilhelm.

"Wilhelm, you are still young. I know that you have made some mistakes, but you can't stay here! They will send you to prison or execute you for your crimes, as I told you back in my office. I have taken the necessary steps to protect your identity, do you understand?" A tear began to flow down Wilhelm's cheek as he looked into his friend's eyes!

CHAPTER 7

The Agency Part 2

It was winter of 1989. America had inaugurated a new president. George H. W. Bush had become the forty-first president of the United States. The Drug Enforcement Agency was making excellent progress on its undercover operation code-named Barracuda.

The telephone started to ring, and the DEA was listening. "John, we need to talk. I have some questions concerning our problem. Meet me at the store tomorrow afternoon at 3:30 p.m."

Jonathan Loveday hung up the phone. He was watching television. He then turned the volume back up using the remote control.

"Who in the hell was that?" Lieutenant Donald Stickles said. Donald was a short fat man with his front teeth missing. He had dark brown eyes. When the lieutenant stared at you, his stare would make a suspect start to snitch. Captain Paul Donovan had ordered Lieutenant Stickles and Agent Steven Enos to stake out John's new Three Eleven Steak House Restaurant. John had just recently opened the restaurant in the West Bridgewater area.

Donna had just walked through the front door as John was hanging up the telephone. "John, who was that?"

"That, Donna, was my new contact. We might have a problem for our next shipment. I need him to take care of some unfinished business."

Donna had gone to the local video rental store. She had rented two movies, *Twins*, starring Arnold Schwarzenegger, and *Rain Man*, starring Tom Cruise. The couple popped some microwave popcorn, and they watched their movies.

The aroma of hot juicy steaks cooking filled the restaurant when he entered through the door. Agent Enos started to make his way to the bar. He had noticed John sitting in a booth next to the entrance, near the kitchen door. Right above his table on the wall hung a portrait of Boston Bruins' Bobby Orr flying through the air after he had scored the winning goal during the 1970 Stanley Cup Game.

"What are you drinking, Mac?" the bartender asked.

"I'll have a Pepsi," Agent Enos replied. Agent Steven Enos was a tall thin man with blond hair. He was a ladies' man. He got a good description of the man that Jonathan Loveday had gone to meet. The man looked like he was of Columbian descent. The two men were really into their conversation. "I wish that I was a fly on the wall," Steve said to himself. He began to browse around the restaurant when he had noticed a waitress bending over cleaning a table that her customers had just left. She was wearing a short skirt; she had very attractive legs. Agent Enos began to stare.

Suddenly, there was a movement that he could see out of the corner of his eye. The man who was talking with Jonathan had gotten up from the table. The two men had started to shake hands. Steve turned his head away from the waitress; he then started to watch the suspects.

Agent Enos took out a five-dollar bill. He then placed it under his glass. He stood up, then he walked to the exit door. Steve quickly made his way to the car when he almost slipped and fell on some snow. The snow was not completely removed from the sidewalk. It had snowed six inches Friday night.

"Well, how did it go?" Lieutenant Stickles asked.

"He met with the contact, and he's leaving now," Steve said. He closed the car door. The suspect had walked out of the restaurant. Lieutenant Stickles quickly picked up the camera. He then started to snap some pictures. You could hear the sound of the camera rapidly taking photographs. The suspect got into a blue Chevy Corvette.

The suspect had put on his sunglasses because the sunlight was very bright. The Corvette turned right at the restaurant exit. The suspect was driving toward the expressway. Lieutenant Donald Stickles and Agent Steven Enos followed him from a distance. Agent Enos said to Donald, "The suspect might be on to us. He's driving very fast." Lieutenant Stickles had agreed with his partner, so he decided to drop back a few more cars. After driving a few miles, the blue Corvette slowed down, so the two DEA agents continued their surveillance as the Corvette drove on to the expressway.

Agent Lisa Crosby started to knock on the door. Her knock got harder and louder. "All right, I'm coming, hold your horses," Agent Allen said. Tom opened the door. When he saw it was Lisa, he let her in. Tom had just woke up. "Lisa, this couldn't wait until we met at the office." Tom turned around. He walked toward his kitchen. "You want some coffee?"

"Yes," Lisa said as she closed the door. Lisa started to walk toward the kitchen, then she noticed Ozzy. Lisa picked him up. She started to rub his head. The cat started to purr. "I'll take cream with two sugars," Lisa said. "Tom, I just found out that Donovan is reassigning me to the Florida Operation, along with Kevin. Did you have anything to do with this?"

"Of course not, Lisa. This is the first that I heard about this." Tom gave Lisa her cup of coffee. She was worried that Tom was getting too attached to Donna. "Lisa, there is absolutely no way that I could or would betray my oath to this agency. I'm just playing my part, so stop worrying about me. You need to concentrate on your assignment." Both agents started to laugh as they drank their coffee. "Lisa, what did you tell Michelle?"

Lisa started to explain to Tom that she told Michelle Bettes that she needed to take some time off because her mother was sick back in California. Lisa also said that she was taking a two-week medical leave. Tom had agreed with Lisa that the excuse that she gave to Michelle was legitimate.

"Lisa, you know that we should have this case wrapped up in less than two weeks!"

Lisa agreed with Tom, and the two of them finished drinking their coffee.

It was a cold day. The temperature was expected to climb into the low twenties. John had left for Florida. He had driven down there this time. Agents Kevin Crainey and Lisa Crosby were hot on his trail. Lisa had died her hair blond. She wore a lot of makeup.

Timothy Ferraro drove into Donna Murphy's driveway. He had almost bumped into her car. Because the sun was very bright, it was shining from behind her house, it had briefly blinded him. He rang the front doorbell. Donna had one of those types of bells that went through several musical chimes. Donna opened the door. "Timmy," she screamed. She then ran out the door to hug him. "What do you have in the bag?" she asked. Timmy started to explain to Donna that he wanted her to put on her jacket and gloves. He told her to meet him in the backyard. Donna did as Timmy asked her to do.

A few minutes later Donna was standing on her patio. "Timmy, are you going to tell me what you have in the bag?" Timmy opened the cloth bag. He then pulled out two pairs of ice skates. Donna started to remind Timmy that she did not how to ice-skate. But Timmy reassured her that nothing bad would happen to her and that he would be with her the whole time. They walked down to the pond. Timmy brought a wooden stool for them to sit on. They then put on their skates.

Timmy and Donna had walked a few feet through the snow. They glided onto the pond. Timmy had his hands on her waist as he was skating backward; he was holding on to Donna. "Don't you let go of me!" she yelled. Soon he was pulling her, and Donna had a big smile on her face. She was skating and laughing. Timmy looked into her beautiful hazel eyes. He was reminiscing about the first day that they met. "Timmy, I'm falling!" Donna had slipped. She then fell onto the ice. She brought Timmy right down with her. He landed right on top of her.

"Are you all right?" he said. Donna was laughing, then Timmy started to laugh too when he had realized that she was okay. Timmy looked into her eyes. He then saw into her soul. They both looked at each other, and they started to kiss each other. They continued to skate for a while longer, but it was cold out. Donna wanted to go back to her house to warm up. Her fingers and ears were starting to get numb. She wanted some hot cocoa.

Timmy was sitting at the kitchen table. Donna was boiling some water to make some hot cocoa. She sat down at the table after she handed Timmy his cocoa. "Timmy, do you remember the first time we met?" Timmy told her that he did. "Tell me about it," Donna said.

"I walked into the nursing home for my job interview, and you were sitting at the nurses' station. You said to me, 'May I help you!'"

Donna stood up from the table. She proceeded to move toward Timmy. Timmy had stood up. She held his hand. Donna led him upstairs to her bedroom. Timmy walked through the door. He noticed that there was a fireplace. Donna's bedroom was enormous. There were some pictures on the mantel, but because of the distance, he could not see who they were. Donna led him toward her bed. She stopped. She then looked Timmy in the eyes. She had given him the look that a woman gives a man when she is ready to be submissive. Timmy remembered how Joanne would give him the same stare when she was in the mood. Timmy knew that Donna was in love with him.

They started to kiss passionately. They removed each other's shirts and stared at each other. Timmy picked her up. He then placed her on the bed. He slowly removed her clothes. He then lay gently on top of her. They made love to each other. When they were finished, Timmy rolled over on the bed. He looked up at the ceiling. "Donna, I think I'm in love with you." Donna turned, and she looked at Timmy. She then kissed him on the cheek.

After a several minutes, Timmy got up. He went to the bathroom. It was connected to the bedroom. When he was finished, he then came out. Donna had fallen asleep. Timmy kissed her on the cheek. He then walked over to the fireplace. Timmy looked at the pictures. That's when he recognized a man who resembled Mr. Rittenberg, but he looked a lot younger. There was a woman and a small girl in the photo.

Timmy had quietly gotten dressed so as not to disturb Donna while she slept. He had gone downstairs to get something to drink. It was the first time that he got the chance to see all of her house. Her home was enormous; he didn't speak because he knew that the DEA was listening. He was walking down the back hallway when he noticed a door that looked very old. Timmy opened the door. There was a long staircase. He noticed a light switch on the side of the wall. Timmy flipped it on.

Timmy reached the bottom of the stairs. There was a lot of cobwebs. He pushed some of them out of the way. He knew that he was in the basement. There were a lot of boxes and old furniture. Timmy saw some boxes on a table in the distance. There was a light above the table. He reached up and pulled the string. The light came on for a few seconds, and then it burnt out. Timmy had noticed that there were other lights like the one near the table. He grabbed a chair, then he started to unscrew one of the lightbulbs. He then went back to the one that was burnt out. Timmy started to replace it. Suddenly, the chair's legs had given out. They collapsed, sending Timmy falling toward the wall. When he hit the wall, it was with such force that it sounded hollow.

Timmy noticed something strange about the wall. He looked a few feet to his right. He saw a small lever protruding out. Timmy pulled it, then the wall opened up. It was a door. Timmy walked into the room. On the side of the wall there was a light switch. He turned it on. Timmy discovered an office. There was a desk near the back wall with several bookshelves filled with books. Timmy started to remove some of the cobwebs out of his way. It looked like no one had been in the room for a very long time.

Timmy proceeded to walk toward the desk. It was covered with dust. But it looked like it had been used in the past. He pulled out the chair. Timmy sat in it. He lifted up the telephone that was on the desk. There was no dial tone. Timmy looked up at the ceiling fan that was in the middle of the room. He then started to go through some of the drawers. There were some medical books. He picked up one and blew off the dust. The title said *Diagnosing Brain Abnormalities*. He then picked up another book and blew off the dust. Timmy started to read it. He was fascinated with the articles. That's when he had heard Donna call his name. Donna was awake. He then quickly put the book in the back of his jeans. Timmy pulled his shirt down over his pants. He then closed the door. Timmy quickly went back to the kitchen.

After stopping in North Carolina for a few hours of rest, Jonathan Loveday was on the move. Agents Kevin Crainey and Lisa Crosby were right on his trail. Kevin was asking Lisa some questions about Tom. She had just moved into the fast lane to pass a garbage truck. They were driving down Interstate 95. Jonathan was about fifty yards ahead of them. "Lisa, do you think Tom is getting too close to Donna?" Lisa started to explain to Kevin that before they had left Boston, she had a talk with Tom. "He swore to me that he was just playing his part," Lisa said.

Jonathan drove into his driveway at his home in Miami. Lisa and Kevin stopped about a block away. Kevin pulled out his binoculars. He observed John entering his house. Lisa called dispatch to send someone over to relieve them. They needed some rest after their long drive.

John opened his front door. He then walked into his kitchen. John opened up his refrigerator. He grabbed a gallon jug of spring water, then he drank some. John picked up his telephone. He had decided to call Donna. "Donna, it's me. I'm at the house. I'll be home Saturday afternoon," he said.

"Okay, John, take care of yourself." John and Donna continued to talk. He then reassured her that this time, they would make enough money to last them a lifetime. Donna wanted John to know that she did not want to continue to live the lifestyle that they were living. They said their good-byes. they both hung up their phones. The DEA was listening.

CHAPTER 8

The Silent Years

He walked into the doctor's office. He then sat down in the waiting area. A nurse spoke to him. "Sir, can I help you?"

He then proceeded to inform her that he had an interview with Dr. Weinstein. She then asked him to sign into the logbook and the doctor would see him as soon as he was finished with his current patient. He then took a seat in the waiting room. There was a copy of the *New York Times*. He picked it up and started to read it.

The gentleman who was sitting next to him asked him, "Do you mind if I read the sports section?" The man wanted to know if the Rangers had won their hockey game the previous night. The New York Rangers had played the Detroit Red Wings at Madison Square Garden. He passed the man the sports section. He then continued to read the day's headlines.

He had come across an article that had intrigued him to the point where his eyes began to bulge out of his head. The newspaper article went on to say, "Yesterday October 15, 1946, at the Nuremberg war trials in Germany, Nazi Hermann Goering was found guilty of crimes against humanity. Hermann was sentenced to death by hanging. But hours before his execution, he committed suicide by poisoning himself. Hermann Goering had cheated the hangman's noose!"

He sat there in shock for a moment, then he said quietly to himself, "He did it, he really committed suicide!" He had looked at the clock on the wall. It said 2:15 p.m. Suddenly the nurse appeared next to him. She then called his name, "Richard Rittenberg, Dr. Weinstein will now see you."

Richard had left from his interview with Dr. Weinstein. He started to walk toward Chambers Street. The clinic where he had his interview was located on Hudson Street. He needed to walk several blocks to reach Chambers Street. Richard had rented a small one-room apartment. He wanted to get home as quickly as possible. He needed to change his clothes. The suit that he was wearing was not appropriate to go out and celebrate with. Dr. Weinstein had decided to take a chance on hiring the younger Dr. Rittenberg. Robert Weinstein was in his early sixties. Robert was a well-liked doctor in the community. He was really impressed with Richard and his knowledge in the medical field. Both men had communicated very well with each other.

The following Monday, Richard was to start as an assistant doctor. It had been twenty-five years since Richard had been living in Manhattan, New York. Dr. Weinstein had retired in 1950. Robert had left the local clinic for Richard to operate. It was a warm spring day in the month of May. Richard was fifty-seven, and he was getting tired of treating people for their medical conditions. His appearance was very remarkable for his age. He had taken very good care of himself. He did not look a day over forty-five.

Richard arrived at work a little earlier than usual. He had made up his mind the previous day that he was going to start living his life. He left his clinic at 6:00 p.m., an hour earlier than his usual time. He had rented a nice apartment off Sixth Avenue. There was a new adult entertainment club that had recently opened not too far from where Richard lived. He had decided that on this Friday night, he was going to go there for some relaxation.

Richard arrived at the club at 9:45 p.m. He had walked through the front doors when he noticed in front of him there were several booths with young men sitting and laughing. The lights in the club were dimmed. There was a stage in the middle of the establishment. Richard looked to his left. About twenty-five feet away there was a bar. He had noticed some women sitting there. They were talking to a group of sailors standing next to them. The girls were laughing. They looked as if they were having a good time. Richard proceeded to walk to the stage. There were metal stools all around it. Just before he got there, to his right was a large man sitting on a chair. The man was well built. He looked like he could take care of himself.

The music was very loud. Richard could barely hear the couple who were laughing as he walked by their table. He continued to walk toward the stage. That's when he had noticed a waitress. She was walking toward him, and she was topless. She was carrying a tray full of beers. Richard began to stare at her breasts. The waitress smiled at Richard. She continued walking by him. She arrived at the table near the front doors where Richard had noticed the young men laughing.

There were a few empty stools on the left side of the stage, so Richard continued walking in that direction. Just as he began to sit down, the woman who was dancing had finished her performance. She was picking up her money that lay on the stage floor. It was given to her by some of the patrons during her dance performance. The record had finally finished playing, and it was quiet for a moment; you could hear people laughing and talking loudly. A waitress had come over to Richard. "Sir, would you like to order something to drink?" Richard stared at her breast for a moment, then he looked at her face. "Yes, I'll have a Heineken!"

While he was talking to the waitress, a man had sat down next him, then Richard turned his head to get a better look at who he was. The man had a Budweiser beer bottle in his hand. He put it on the table. He then reached into his shirt pocket, and he pulled out a pack of Winston cigarettes. He then proceeded to light one. The lights on the stage got a little bit dimmer, then a song started to play. The disc jockey said the song was called "Jumping Jack Flash," then the disc jockey announced, "Give it up for Monica," like the song title had stated that's what she was doing. Monica had exploded onto the stage.

She was wearing a see-through purple negligee with black panties, and she could dance. Right away Richard found himself following her every move that she would make. Richard had liked what he was looking at. Monica was a very attractive woman. She had red hair and a beautiful smile. Monica had finished her performance. Richard took a fifty-dollar bill from his wallet. He then wrote a message on it. He gave her the money when she had come over to his side of the stage as she was gathering money that was thrown on the floor while she was performing her routine.

Monica left the stage area. She then went to her dressing room. She sat down at her booth. Monica put her money on her table. She then started counting it. Her friend who was sitting next to her began to talk with her. "Wow, they must have really liked you."

"I did pretty well," Monica said. She then reached for her bottle of water. Monica started drinking. That's when she looked at herself in the mirror. Monica thought about the day when she would no longer have to take her clothes off for a crowd of drunken men. She then noticed the fifty-dollar bill, and there was writing on it. "I would like to meet you, I am sitting on the left side of the stage. I am wearing a dark blue shirt." She then started laughing.

"What's so funny?" her friend asked.

"This guy, he wants to meet me. He wrote it on my fifty-dollar bill that he gave me."

She had walked over to where Richard was sitting. "Hi!"

Richard had turned around with a puzzled look on his face. "Do I know you?" he said.

"It's me, Monica." Richard didn't recognize her because her hair was black, not red. She explained to him that was her wig and part of her costume.

"Would you like to sit at a table?" Richard asked. They both walked over to a table not too far from the stage. Richard had noticed the man with the huge muscles he had noticed earlier was paying close attention to them. They both sat down. They each started to speak. "I'm Richard," he said. "My name is Barbara." They both shook hands as they began to talk. Richard understood that Monica was her stage name. "Who's the big guy that keeps staring at me? Is he your boyfriend?"

"No, silly. He's Eddie, the bouncer." Richard started to laugh, and so did Barbara. They talked for at least thirty minutes. Barbara had agreed to stop by the clinic on Monday for a lunch date with Dr. Rittenberg.

Barbara kept her word. She had arrived at the medical clinic. The two went to a Chinese restaurant. They really enjoyed each other's company. They had just finished eating when Barbara asked Richard how old he was. Richard then told her his age, but she didn't believe him. Barbara had opened her purse. She took out a cigarette, then she lit it.

"How old are you, Barbara?"

"I'm forty-two, Richard."

Barbara was really excited at the prospect of Richard and their getting to know each other better. They began to date, and after several weeks, they had dinner again. That's when Barbara began to open up to Richard. She wanted him to know more about herself. She told him that she was a widow. Barbara had lost her husband a few years ago in Vietnam. He was a staff sergeant for the Marine Corps. He was ten years younger than her. He had his life cut short. He had stepped on a land mine in a rice paddy; he was killed instantly. "Richard, I have a daughter. Would you like to meet her?" Barbara invited Richard over for dinner Saturday evening.

Richard continued to listen to her talk about her past while he looked into her hazel eyes. Richard had understood what she was going through. Richard began to reminisce the day when he was informed that Marlene, Kateland, Karl, and Gilda were killed at the Berlin movie theater.

The doorbell had rung at Barbara's apartment. She yelled, "The door is open." Richard walked in, and he saw Barbara walking toward him. He then pulled out from behind his back a bouquet of flowers. He then proceeded to give them to her. Her daughter had run to meet Richard, and he said, "What's your name, pretty lady?"

"Madonna Anne Murphy." Richard had asked Madonna, if she didn't mind if he could call her Donna.

The year was 1972. Richard had turned sixty. He decided that he wanted to retire. Richard and Barbara had developed a wonderful relationship together. They had decided that it was time to leave New York. Richard bought a nice house in Barbara's name. They moved to a private wooded neighborhood in Carver, Massachusetts. They quickly settled into their new Victorian-style home, and they were very happy about living in a small town. Richard and Barbara did not miss the city. Life in the country was marvelous.

The day was July 29, 1982. Richard was quietly celebrating his birthday. He had turned seventy. He was reflecting on his life. Richard started to remember his childhood. Richard began to reflect about his years in the Nazi party. It had seemed like yesterday, he had thought to himself. He grabbed the cable remote, then he sat down on the couch. He pressed the on button. Richard started to channel surf. He came across this particular channel. When he saw a lot of people sitting in a stadium, he thought to himself, that must be a soccer game. But as the camera's view had started to widen, it showed a stage with people standing on it. Richard said to himself, "A stupid rock concert!"

Just before Richard changed the channel, a voice came out of the television. "God loves you!" The speaker on the stage said, "God loves you today." Those very words that were spoken, they had begun to stir up a feeling in Richard's spirit that he had never felt before. Richard turned up the volume. He then continued to listen. "God loves you. He will forgive you of your past sins today. You see, He sent His Son Jesus to the cross to pay the penalty for all of your sins and my sins. Today, I encourage you to accept His offer and invite Jesus Christ into your life today. Right where you are, you can say a simple prayer like this."

Richard started to repeat the prayer: "Lord, I ask that you come into my life and forgive me of my sins. Help me to serve you, help me to find peace in my life. Amen!"

Richard started to weep uncontrollably. He finally was able to forgive himself. Richard knew that he had caused a lot of pain and suffering toward his fellow men. On August 18, 1982, Richard was living life from a new perspective. He was really enjoying life for the first time in a long time. Richard had the same type of joy when he had first met his deceased wife, Marlene. Barbara was a loyal companion. She was an excellent mother. Richard Rittenberg cared for her deeply.

Richard really loved Donna. She was the daughter that he never got the chance to have. He really cherished her very dearly. Richard had decided to work on his project. He was on his way to his secret office. He started to make his way down the stairs. That's when he felt a very sharp pain inside of his head. It had felt as if his skull was about to explode. Richard had fallen to the bottom of the stairs. When he landed on the basement floor, he broke his right hip and arm. Richard Rittenberg had a major stroke. It had left him in a semivegetative state.

Barbara was devastated. She had gone into a state of depression. She then started to drink and smoke at an alarming rate. Her health continued to deteriorate drastically. In the year 1985, she had developed lung cancer, and her left lung was removed. Barbara's doctor had told her that she only had a few months to live because her right lung was failing rapidly. Her priest had given Barbara her last rites, and he was leaving her hospital room. Donna had left early from the college that she was attending. She had been in her nursing class when she received a message from the staff that her mother was receiving her last rites.

"Father," Donna said when she called out to the priest. He was closing the door to her mother's room when Donna had arrived at the hospital. "How is she?" asked Madonna.

"Go and see her, my daughter," the priest said.

Donna stood at the door. She took a deep breath. She gathered her composure. She then went into the room to see her mother. Donna had greeted her mother. She leaned over the bed. She then kissed her on the cheek. Donna Murphy then began to cry.

"Don't cry, Madonna, I need you to be strong." Barbara went on to tell her daughter that she had some important information concerning her stepfather. "Listen to me very carefully, Madonna. I am about to tell you some information about Richard. You must promise me that you will take care of him. Your father was born in Germany during a time when the world was different than the world we now live in. He was a doctor for the Nazis. A friend helped him to escape to the United States so that he would avoid war crime charges against him. You must never let anyone know this. Please remember, sweetheart, it was Richard that rescued us from a life of poverty and misery. He took care of us, and we owe him our love. Promise me that you will protect him."

Madonna looked into her mother's eyes, and with tears flowing from her eyes, she said, "I promise, Mother!" Barbara looked at Donna and smiled. She closed her eyes. She then passed away. Donna wept bitterly as she screamed, shook, and yelled for her mother to wake up.

CHAPTER 9

He Was about to Betray His Oath

Agents Stickles and Enos had followed the suspect from the Three Eleven Steak House Restaurant. The blue Corvette had exited the expressway, and it was stopped at a red light. Agent Enos started to reminisce about the waitress back at the restaurant. Suddenly, Donald stepped on the gas when the light turned green. The suspect was on the move. The two agents were following him from a distance. The man had driven to a warehouse on the east side in Boston, near the shipping yards. Donald and Steven headed back to division headquarters in downtown Boston.

Captain Donovan had sat down at his desk. He was going through the stack of reports that had piled up on his desk. He started to read Agent Crosby's report. She had written that she was concerned that Agent Allen might be getting too close to suspect Donna Murphy.

Tom was sitting at his desk when he had heard the captain. "Agent Allen, get in my office!" Captain Donovan informed Tom that he was taking him off Operation Barracuda. The captain gave Tom the excuse that he had felt the agent was getting too personal with suspect Donna Murphy. This was his decision. Agent Allen began to question the captain's decision, but Paul interrupted Tom; he had explained to Tom that he didn't want to hear any more about it. Captain Paul Donovan gave Agent Thomas Allen the rest of the day off. Tom then left the captain's office. He had an expression of anger on his face.

"Damn it, Lisa," he said. Tom then sat down at his desk just as Lieutenant Stickles and Agent Enos returned. Donald immediately sent the film that they had taken of the suspect from the restaurant to the agency's photo lab for developing.

Donald and Steve were inside the captain's office. They were sitting at the command table. They were discussing their case when the photos arrived from the lab. "Any idea who this man is?" Captain Donovan said. The two agents responded with a no. Captain Donovan then asked Lieutenant Stickles to check with the Immigration Department to see if he could find out why the suspect was here in Boston.

Agent Allen had left the precinct. He was walking to the parking garage. He then got into his Camaro. Tom was driving home. Tom was very upset at what just happened, but he had realized that the captain was right. He had just turned on his car radio when a song started to play. Thomas Allen began to sing out loud the words. "I have climbed highest mountain, I have run through the fields only to be with you, only to be with you. I have run, I have crawled, I have scaled these city walls, these city walls, only to be with you. But I still, haven't found what I'm looking for." Tom started to sing louder the words to the song, and the longer the song played, the louder he yelled. Agent Thomas Allen knew that he did find what he was looking for.

Tom had noticed Donna's smile the first time he had looked into her hazel eyes. Thomas Allen knew in his heart that she was his soul mate. Agent Thomas Allen was in love.

Tom arrived at his house. He had just walked through his front door. Ozzy was there waiting for him when he entered through his door. Tom bent over and then picked Ozzy up. "What a good kitty you are." Tom rubbed his head. He then set him down, then went to the kitchen. "Are you hungry?" Ozzy began to rub himself against Tom's legs. He knew that the cat wanted to eat. So he fed him a can of 9 Lives tuna and egg dinner. While Ozzy was eating his food, Tom sat down on his couch. He then grabbed the cable remote. He then

HE WAS ABOUT TO BETRAY HIS OATH

turned to a music video channel. Tom watched a couple of videos. Then he decided to change the channel to Channel 7. The news anchor was announcing that there was a double homicide at the waterfront. Emily Lopez was standing by.

"Good evening, folks. I'm Emily Lopez. I am reporting to you from the Back Bay. There has been a double homicide this afternoon. Two men were discovered by this person standing to my right talking with this police officer."

The camera started to shift from Emily to the witness and the police officer. Emily went on to say, "The victims were identified as Boston mafia associates Jeffrey Gates and Raymond Sierra. They were found shot to death inside that car to my left!"

The camera then started to show a black Lincoln parked in front of a brick building. Emily went on to say, "As you can see, the car is riddled with bullet holes. We have talked with other witnesses who have said that they saw a blue Chevy Corvette speeding away from the area!" The camera now zoomed on to Emily. "Live from the Back Bay, this is Emily Lopez, Channel 7 News, reporting. Back to you, Peter."

Jonathan Loveday had been really active in Miami. He was spending a lot of time at a warehouse and his restaurant. He was finalizing his major drug deals with the Columbian drug cartel. They were smuggling large shipments of cocaine into the country. They were moving it up to the Boston area. John was using his restaurant chain to accomplish this task. The Columbians had switched operations from the Bahamas to the island of Aruba.

The United States Coast Guard had been squeezing the cartel with the US "Just Say No" campaign. The cocaine was being shipped in large coffee containers in Aruba. They were placing them in large cargo ships that were headed to shipping ports in Florida. The US Customs Agency didn't have a clue as to what was happening. But the Drug Enforcement Agency was watching. Operation Barracuda was winding down.

Agents Kevin Crainey and Lisa Crosby were outside of John's Miami residence. They had to park a little closer than previously. The two agents were almost in front of his house. There was a social gathering going on across the street. The people who were visiting John's neighbor had parked in their usual spot. Kevin and Lisa were monitoring John's phone line through a listening device that was connected to a wireless transmitter. John's phone started to ring. When he answered it, the voice said, "You won't be hearing from Gates and Sierra anymore. That problem has been resolved!"

"Excellent, Carlos. I will have your funds wired to your Cayman Islands account," John said. John started to hang up the phone, but before he placed it on its receiver, Jonathan heard a clicking sound. It had aroused his curiosity. So he went to his front window, and he looked out. Jonathan saw an unmarked police cruiser sitting at the end of his house. John quickly went to his bedroom. He then grabbed his binoculars. He zoomed in on the vehicle. Right away he knew that he was being watched. John needed to figure out what to do next. Jonathan Loveday went into his garage. He walked over to his maintenance drawer. John pulled out some light switch timers, and he placed one in his bedroom. Then he set the delay switch timer for the light to turn on at 4:40 p.m. and shut off at 1:00 a.m.

Then Jonathan went to the living room. He then set the other light timer there. He programmed the switch delay to turn on at 5:00 p.m. and shut off at 11:00 p.m. He then looked at his watch. It said 11:45 a.m. John snuck out the back door. He climbed over his fence. He then ran across his neighbor's yard. John ran as fast as he could for at least a mile. He then started to get tired, so he started to walk. Jonathan Loveday looked over his shoulder. There was no one following him.

Tom had gone into his bedroom after he had finished watching the news. He picked up the book that he had taken from the hidden room at Donna's house. Tom opened it up, and he started reading it.

Log entry 7/29/40

Dear God, what have I done? I have helped in the systematic killings of innocent Jewish people. Hitler has gone mad. I don't want to be a part of his madness anymore. I need to figure out what to do. Today is my birthday. I watched my beautiful wife and daughter arrive home safely from the marketplace.

Tom couldn't believe what he was reading. His adrenaline started to flow throughout his body. Tom kept on reading log entry after entry.

Log entry 7/29/45

Today, I met with Reich Marshal Goering. He looked very frail. I could not believe what my eyes were seeing. But I knew it was him when he spoke; it was Hermann!

Tom kept reading out loud.

I made a deal with him that I would help him commit suicide. In return, Hermann gave me some directions to a Lake where there are millions of dollars of gold coins and bars!

Tom had read about Hermann Goering's lust for art and gold. Tom had been fascinated with the history of World War II since he first started to learn about the history of the United States, during his training at the Great Lakes Naval Academy. The Nazis had looted gold and art from the countries that they had occupied. Tom kept reading the journal. It had said that around thirty miles outside of the city of Hannover, there was a large reservoir. Follow Leinefeld Road, it runs parallel to the lake; there is a large water tower on the left side of the road. About five hundred feet past the tower, there is a long dirt road to your right. Follow it to the end. About one hundred yards out, on the bottom of the lake, you will find a brass chest the size of a coffin filled with gold. "Eureka!" Tom yelled. He jumped up and down in his bedroom, screaming, "I'm rich, I am rich!"

It was Monday. Donna Murphy went to work. She noticed that Laura and Timmy were not there. She asked Michelle Bettes, who was the director of nursing. Michelle had explained to Donna that Laura had some personal family business to take care of and that she took a two-week leave of absence. Donna then heard Harry whistling, and she knew that he was walking toward her.

"Harry, is Timmy coming to work today?"

"Donna, he left me a message. He said that he quit."

Donna's heart sank to the bottom of her stomach. Donna could not believe that he would abandon her so fast. She had started to cry. It was at that moment that Donna Murphy realized that she had fallen in love with Timothy Ferraro. Donna Murphy quickly gathered her composure. She started to make her rounds. She needed to deliver medicine to her patients. Donna walked into room 218. She walked up to her father, and when he saw her, he tried to smile. But he couldn't. He was having a bad day. Some days are better than other days.

"Good morning, Daddy." She leaned over the bed and kissed him. Donna took his vital signs and checked his feeding tube. She then tucked his pillow under his head. Donna then left the room.

Agent Allen woke up a little earlier than usual. He did not sleep very well last night. He went through his morning routine. Tom decided to leave for work a little bit early. Thomas was walking to the front door entrance when he saw Lorenzo, the homeless man, standing at his usual spot, soliciting for money. "Here you go, Lorenzo. Take this dollar and go buy a cup of coffee before I have you arrested!"

"Thank you, Detective." Lorenzo took the dollar. He then started to leave, then Tom walked through the front entrance. He put his gun and badge on the conveyor belt. Tom proceeded to walk through the metal detector. Tom then took a few moments to talk with Ralph, the security guard. Tom started to walk down the hallway toward the elevators. He passed by the Photo and Documentation Department. Tom stuck his head inside the door. "Good morning, Rebecca." Rebecca smiled, and she blushed. "Good morning to you too, Agent Allen." Tom gave Rebecca her usual compliments. Agent Thomas Allen told her just how lovely she looked. Tom arrived at his desk. He was going through his mail. He also was preparing for his next assignment. He had some typing to do. There was a lot of paperwork that needed to be done. Tom looked up at the clock; it said 9:15 a.m. Tom began to ponder how Lisa and Kevin were doing on their stakeout.

HE WAS ABOUT TO BETRAY HIS OATH

Tom looked at Lisa's desk. It was collecting dust. He had missed her smile. He started to type again, then he pulled the paper out of the typewriter. He then looked at it. The top of the form had the name Donna Murphy on it. Tom started to think about the day when they had gone ice-skating and the joy that she had on her face. "Agent Allen, get in my office!" Tom got up, and he walked into the captain's office.

"Yes, Captain."

"I'm temporarily putting you back on Operation Barracuda. Stickles is tied up for most of the day. I need you to work with Steve."

Tom walked down to the end of the room where Agent Enos's desk was located. Agent Enos told Tom to have a seat, and he would bring him up to date on Operation Barracuda. He said, "Carlos Ortega was responsible for the double homicide at the waterfront. John had hired him for the hit. Carlos works for the cartel. We are now calling in the Feds to assist us with this operation. This has now turned into racketeering and extortion, along with murder. The Federal Bureau of Investigation has more agents and resources. Tom, we're about to get indictments from a federal grand jury to execute search warrants on Jonathan Loveday and his girlfriend, Donna Murphy. Along with various members of the Columbian drug cartel operating in the United States." Agent Thomas Allen was not listening to Agent Steven Enos. He had stopped when he had heard the name Donna Murphy.

Agent Thomas Allen knew he had to do something. He just could not stand by and let the DEA take away the woman that he loved. Tom quickly made his way back to his desk. He started typing out some documents and forms. Agent Johnson had walked past his desk when he asked Tom, "How are you doing?" Tom acknowledged him. He then glanced at the clock. It said 11:05 a.m. Tom then picked up the telephone. He started dialing a number.

"Federal Bureau of Investigation, Philadelphia Division, Melissa speaking. How may I direct your call?"

"This is Agent Thomas Allen of the Drug Enforcement Agency, Boston Division. Identification number 10422108."

"Yes, Agent Allen, how may I direct your call?"

"I need to speak with Special Agent Brian Singer."

"One moment. Please hold while I transfer your call!"

Brian Singer did not reenlist in the navy. Like Tom, he also had decided to work for the Justice Department. "Agent Allen, how are you doing, buddy?" Brian and Tom talked for a few minutes about their days in the navy and their present jobs. "So what can I do for you?" Brian asked.

"I am investigating a case. I was wondering if you could do a background check for me?"

"On whom?" Special Agent Singer asked.

"On a gentleman who went by the name of Wilhelm Strausvon, possible alias Richard Rittenberg, born in Germany, July 29, 1912! Immigrated to the United States sometime in August 1945."

Brian told Tom that he would search the FBI archives. The two agents continued to talk for a while. Tom told Brian that he would call him back later during the day.

Tom finished typing his documents. He also put them in a folder. He then proceeded to the elevator. The door had opened, and Lieutenant Stickles was walking out. "Lieutenant," Tom said. The lieutenant was in a hurry. He just glared at Tom when they passed each other. Tom got on the elevator. He was headed to the Photo Documentation Department. Tom walked through the door, and Rebecca was sitting at her desk. She looked up, and she smiled at Tom. Rebecca wanted Tom to know that she was there to help him anytime. She was a heavyset woman. But she was as sweet as she could be, and Becky adored Agent Thomas Allen.

"Becky, I need you to notarize these forms and stamp these passports."

"Sure, Tom," Rebecca said. While she was completing the task that Tom had asked her to do, he liked to flirt with her. Tom knew it made her feel wanted, but on this particular reason, he wanted to keep her occupied so that she would not pay attention to what she was doing. "Really now, Thomas, what has come over you?" Tom had his arms around her waist, and he was nibbling on her earlobe. Becky continued to blush while Tom worked his charm.

HE WAS ABOUT TO BETRAY HIS OATH

Tom then left Rebecca's office and the division. He headed to the parking garage. Agent Thomas Allen knew that time was getting short, and he needed to accomplish a few more tasks. He knew that he had to get moving because he was about to betray his oath.

Tom arrived at his house. He knew that he needed to move fast. Tom was determined to cover his tracks. He knew that the DEA would stop at nothing to find him. He packed a few personal items and put some food in his cat's bowl. Tom hurried out the door. He was on his way to a federal bank. He wanted to open a Swiss bank account in someone else's name. He then went to a pay phone and contacted Special Agent Brian Singer. Brian had confirmed what Tom asked him earlier. Tom now knew that Donna's stepfather was actually a former Nazi. The stories in his journal were true. He hung up the phone. He then made several other important telephone calls.

"The diary," Tom mumbled. He was driving to Donna's house when he realized that he had forgotten it. Tom knew that it was too late to go back and retrieve it. "Man, you sure do smell," Tom said to his passenger. He was riding with him. Tom let down his passenger side window a little bit. He had to turn the heat up a little more. It was cold outside. Tom looked at the time. It said 4:12 p.m. He knew Donna was home.

They finally arrived at Donna's house. Tom didn't know how she would react, but his love for her overwhelmed him. "You sit tight and don't get out of this car," Tom said to his passenger. He then opened his door, and he got out of the car. He then looked at Donna's house, took a deep breath, then he walked to the front door.

Tom rang the doorbell. It proceeded to go through various musical tones. "Timmy," Donna said. When she opened the door, she then went outside to hug him. Tom quietly told her that he had some very important information that he needed to tell her. He told Donna that he had to do something. He also wanted her not to speak. Tom walked into the kitchen. Donna followed him. He then went to the cabinet, took out a glass, and filled it with water. Tom then proceeded to walk to the living room on the side of the grandfather clock that was facing the wall. Tom pulled the listening device off. He then dropped it into the glass. Tom and Donna then went to the bathroom. Donna had a puzzled look on her face. Tom reached underneath the front of the vanity. He then pulled the bug off. Tom dropped it into the toilet. Tom then emptied the glass into the toilet; he flushed it. He wiped off the outside of the glass. He then set it on the top of the toilet.

"Timmy, what in the world is going on?"

"My name is not Timmy. My real name is Thomas Allen!"

"But I don't understand," Donna said.

Tom went on to explain to Donna that he was a federal agent with the Drug Enforcement Agency. "Donna, the United States government is getting ready to arrest you and Jonathan for drug trafficking, extortion, and murder!"

Donna had started to cry. She knew what Tom was telling her was true. "Don't cry, Donna. That's why I am here. I love you, Donna. I am willing to betray the oath that I have sworn to, to save you! I have worked out a plan, but first I need to ask you a serious question. Do you love me?"

Donna began to wipe away her tears, then she looked Tom in the eye. "Yes, Thomas, I do." They began to kiss and comfort each other. Tom and Donna then went upstairs to pack some of her personal belongings. While Donna was packing, Tom went on to explain to her where they were going. He told her that they would be leaving the United States and that they were traveling to West Germany. Donna then stopped packing. She had a look of concern on her face. "Don't worry about your father. He will be just fine."

"You know about Richard?" Tom told Donna that the government was not interested in prosecuting a seventy-six-year-old former Nazi who is a paraplegic and who entered this country with the help of the Justice Department. It would be a complete embarrassment to the present administration. Donna then smiled while she continued to pack her suitcase.

Tom's passenger was sitting in the car waiting for him to return. He was getting very agitated. It was cold outside. He needed to go to the bathroom. His bladder was about to explode. He remembered what Agent Thomas Allen said, he then said an explicit word, got out of the car. He ran through the little bit of snow that was on the ground and made his way to the end of the house. There were some evergreen shrubs that he could use for cover. Just as he was finishing, a car pulled into the driveway. The car's headlights had briefly shone on him, but he quickly ducked behind the tree to cover himself. He had peeked through some of the branches and saw that it was a yellow cab. There was a tall man, well built, standing there without a coat, talking to the taxi driver. The man then proceeded to walk up the driveway while the taxi started to back out of the driveway. The man stopped and looked at the blue Camaro. He then put his hand on the hood of the car. He said an explicit word. He then turned and walked to the front door.

Donna and Tom were finishing up in the bedroom. Tom had started to close her suitcase when she screamed, "Stop!" Donna ran over to the fireplace to take the picture of her mother and Richard along with her when she was six. "I can't believe that I almost left this behind." She then paused at the mantel for a brief moment.

Donna then turned. She then gave the picture to Tom. He placed it in the suitcase. Tom had shut the light off. They had started to walk down the stairs. Just as they reached the bottom, the front door opened up. It was Jonathan Loveday. "Hold it right there," Tom yelled as he took out his gun and pointed it at John. John put his hands up, and he looked at Donna. "What the hell is going on?" John said. Again, Tom told him to shut up and to keep his hands raised. Tom put down the suitcase. He started to move closer to John. Just when Tom was ready to apprehend him, the grandfather clock began to chime. It was 6:00 p.m., and the old antique clock really let you know that half of the day was over.

John took advantage of Tom's misfortune. You see, Tom was distracted for a brief moment. John grabbed Tom's arm. The two men began to wrestle. A shot was fired from Tom's gun. A bullet went into the wall, right next to the painting of Baron Manfred von Richthofen. He was also known by the name the Red Baron, a German fighter pilot during World War I. John punched Tom in the stomach, causing him to let go of the weapon. The two men had fallen to the floor, and they started rolling around, each man trying to get the upper hand. Jonathan managed to break free. He was trying to reach for Tom's gun.

Tom grabbed John's leg and pulled him down. He then climbed on top of him. He started to punch him in the face. John then used his upper body strength to push Tom off him. John then rolled on top of Tom. He had started to choke him. Tom was gagging for air. His face started to turn blue. Donna started to yell at John to stop it. "You're killing him." She then picked up the gun. It had fallen next to her. She was ready to shoot Jonathan in the back, but Donna could not pull the trigger. She thought about her unborn baby, and she realized that he was its father. Donna, being from a Catholic background, could not find it within herself to murder John. But she knew that she still had to do something; the situation was getting serious. The man that she loved was beginning to lose consciousness. She looked over to the corner table. There was a glass vase filled with flowers. Donna threw away the flowers. She then picked up the vase. Donna proceeded to walk toward John As she was approaching him, she could see that Tom had a very concerned look on his face. Donna smashed the vase on the back of John's head. Jonathan fell sideways to the floor.

"Are you all right?" Donna asked as she bent over to help Tom up from the floor. Tom was coughing and gasping for air. He started to breathe again. Tom's face started to get some color back. "Is he dead?" Donna asked. Tom was bending over to check John's pulse. He had some blood dripping from the back of his head. "Donna, you just knocked him out." Tom started to stagger as he walked toward the suitcase. Donna held on to him. They left the house. They started walking toward Tom's car. "Damn it," Tom said.

"What is it?" Donna asked.

"I told him to stay in the car."

"Told who?" Donna yelled.

"Lorenzo," replied Tom. "Lorenzo, Lorenzo!" Tom yelled.

He answered when he came out from behind the bushes. As Lorenzo got closer to Tom and Donna, he could see that Tom was in a fight. "Are you all right, Detective?" Tom told him to shut up and get in the backseat of the car. Tom then put Donna's suitcase in the back hatch, next to his.

The social gathering was winding down across the street from John's house. Agent Crainey had moved his car back to his usual spot. Kevin and Lisa were waiting for Agent Chris Gilmartin to take over surveillance. It was a little past 4:00 p.m., and Chris was late.

Agents Kevin Crainey and Lisa Crosby had been spending a lot of time together. This was their first assignment. They both realized that they had a lot in common. They agreed to meet each other at the hotel's restaurant after agent Gilmartin had relieved them from their surveillance.

They both had freshened up. Lisa wore a black dress that really altered her appearance. When Kevin saw her, he was sitting at the table and he almost did not recognize her. "You look totally astonishing," Kevin said while he got up from his chair, and he quickly went around the table to where Lisa was standing. Kevin pulled out her chair. She proceeded to sit in it. "Thank you," Lisa said. Kevin went back to his seat. They began to talk. Kevin knew that Lisa had dressed this way for him to notice her. He understood when a woman was seeking affection. They continued to talk for a little while until the waitress came over to take their orders. They ordered some food and drinks. They were feeling real good about themselves. The next thing that they both knew was that they were riding up the hotel elevator, and they were embraced in each other's arms. They were kissing passionately. Kevin had his hands all over Lisa, then Lisa started to get aroused.

Suddenly, the elevator had stopped, then the door started to open. An older couple had gotten onto the elevator. The man pushed the button to the floor that they were going to. The elderly man had looked at Lisa. He then noticed that her slip was showing. Lisa was discretely trying to pull down her skirt. The man then noticed she was blushing. He then looked at Kevin. He had given Kevin a wink with his left eye. The elderly man then smiled. Kevin and Lisa had arrived at Lisa's room. They both entered through the door together;

they were holding hands. Lisa pulled Kevin closer to the bed. They both started to kiss each other again. They removed each other's clothes. Kevin picked her up, and he placed her on the bed, where they made love to each other.

Tom, Donna, and Lorenzo were driving on the expressway heading back to Boston. They were on their way to the Greyhound bus station. The car radio was playing. Donna asked Tom to change the station. There was a heavy metal song playing. She didn't particularly care for that type of music. "Go ahead, change the channel," Tom said. Donna then started to channel surf. When she had heard a song that she liked, Donna started to sing with the lyrics. "Music can be such a revelation, dancing around you feel the sweet sensation, we might be lovers if the rhythm's right. I hope this feeling never ends tonight, only when I'm dancing can I feel this free. At night, I lock the doors where no one else can see, I'm tired of dancing here all by myself. Tonight I want to dance with someone else!"

Donna had turned down the volume, then she looked at Tom. "Did you know that my name is Madonna?" Tom turned, and he looked into her hazel eyes. Tom said, "I love you, Madonna Anne Murphy."

Tom pulled into the bus terminal. Tom then parked his car as far back as he could from the bus station entrance. The three of them walked through the terminal entrance door. Tom told Lorenzo and Donna to wait by the entrance door. Agent Thomas Allen proceeded to walk to the ticket booth, where he bought two tickets. Tom went back to where Donna and Lorenzo were waiting. "Here you go, Lorenzo, just like I promised you, a one-way ticket to a warmer city."

"Thanks, Detective." Lorenzo took the ticket and some money that Tom gave him, then Lorenzo walked to the bus terminal. Agent Thomas Allen and Donna Murphy started to walk down to the long corridor that led to an entrance to the top of the street. Tom tore up the other ticket, then he tossed it into the waste receptacle. They climbed some stairs that went up to the street. When they walked through the door, they were standing on the sidewalk. Donna started to stare at the skyscrapers. The buildings towered so high up in the sky. It had been a while since Madonna had been in the city of Boston. At night the buildings had all their lights on. They were so tall. They looked so pretty, she had thought.

There was a lot of traffic, and you could hear the noise from all the automobiles driving around throughout the city. There were people walking down the sidewalks. The wind was blowing very heavily. The sky was clear, and it was cold. Donna didn't have any gloves on, so she unzipped her suitcase, then she took some out. "Taxi," Tom yelled. He was trying to hail a yellow cab. It pulled up to the curb. The driver then jumped out of the vehicle, then he proceeded to put their luggage into the trunk. Tom and Donna got into the backseat. "Where to?" the cabdriver said.

"JFK International Airport," replied Tom.

"Logan International is right around the corner," the man said. He had a Jamaican accent, but Tom insisted that he drive to New York. Tom promised him that he would make it worth his time if he drove there. The taxi driver called his dispatch and informed them that he was headed to New York. It was close to 1:00 a.m. Tom had looked at his watch. He then whispered to himself, "We're right on schedule." Tom looked over at Donna. She was leaning up against him. Donna was falling asleep.

"Driver, pull into the parking lot of Sam's Motel," Tom said. The motel was a few miles away from JFK Airport. Tom paid his fare, then he gave the driver a two-hundred-dollar tip. The taxi driver was grateful, and he thanked Tom for his generosity. Agent Thomas Allen rented a room under his new name. He and Donna settled down for the rest of the night.

It was 8:00 a.m. Captain Donovan was yelling to his agents. "Where is Agent Allen?" he asked. Agent Enos had just walked into his office. Lieutenant Stickles was sitting in a chair. The captain wanted them to focus. They were about to serve warrants at 10:00 a.m. Steven told the captain he didn't know where Tom was. Paul Donovan wanted his men to head to the nursing home and to the Murphy residence. The FBI agents would be serving both restaurants and warehouses in Massachusetts and Florida. Agents Crainey and Crosby were going to serve Jonathan Loveday at his house.

"Gentlemen, let's shut down Operation Barracuda," Captain Paul Donovan said.

Kevin and Lisa were driving to Jonathan Loveday's house to serve their warrants. Agent Gilmartin had hung around. He wanted in on the action. "Not one word," Lisa said. She turned on the siren and blue lights. She then stepped on the gas pedal, and the car sped through the red light. Kevin just looked at her, and he smiled. Kevin was not about to forget Lisa was awesome, he thought to himself.

The agents pulled up to John's house. They were joined by some Florida State Police. They entered the home. "Clear," Lisa said. She put her firearm back into its holster. Jonathan Loveday was gone. Kevin and Chris quickly started to blame each other.

Lisa had to yell at them to stop acting like children. They all knew that Captain Paul Donovan was going to be pissed, and someone's head was going to roll. They started to gather evidence. Lisa had gone outside to the car to radio dispatch that John had escaped. Agents Enos and Johnson, along with two other agents, drove over to the Murphy residence to execute their warrants. Lieutenant Stickles and some Massachusetts State Police went to the nursing home.

Agent Enos was the first to enter the house. Some Carver Police Units had arrived to secure the perimeter. Agent Enos noticed that there had been some kind of struggle in the foyer by the stairs. The agents quickly remained alert as they walked inside the home. Steve had noticed blood on the floor leading up the stairs. Agents Enos and Johnson followed the trail. They made their way down the hallway. Steve opened the bedroom door. He shined his flashlight into the room, then saw a suspect lying on the bed. He motioned to his partner. "Freeze," Steve yelled. There was no movement. Steve moved closer to the bed. He then realized it was Jonathan Loveday. He had lost a lot of blood, but he was still breathing. The DEA agents summoned an ambulance.

Captain Donovan had received updates from all his agents in the field on Operation Barracuda. His gut feeling told him that Agent

Allen was behind the disappearance of suspect Donna Murphy. He was discussing this with Lieutenant Stickles, but Paul needed proof. He filed the necessary paperwork for a search warrant to Agent Allen's house. He desperately wanted to keep this out of the media for as long as possible. Captain Paul Donovan summoned Agents Kevin Crainey and Lisa Crosby back from Florida.

Kevin and Lisa were at the Miami International Airport waiting to catch their flight back to Boston. "There goes the warm weather and sunshine," Lisa said. They had boarded their plane, and it took off. The pilot leveled the airplane to cruising altitude. Flight restrictions were suspended. Flight attendants started to make their cabin rounds. One of the attendants was pushing her drink cart when she had arrived to where Lisa and Kevin were sitting. She said, "Would you like something to drink?" Kevin stared at her breasts, and then he looked at her name tag. It said Sharon. "Yes, ma'am, I'll have a Sprite!" While the stewardess poured his soda, Kevin began to undress her with his eyes. That's when Lisa punched him in the shoulder. "Do I detect some jealousy?" Kevin said. "Shut up and drink your soda, you need to cool off!" She then smirked at Kevin.

Tom had woken up a little bit earlier than Donna. He had a lot on his mind. He knew that they still were not safe. Thomas Allen understood how the government worked, and it was just a matter of time before they realize he'd gone AWOL. Tom knew that he was a fugitive, and if he got caught, he would spend the rest of his life in a federal prison. He understood the urgent need for him and Donna to get out of the country as soon as possible. He wished that there was an earlier flight to West Germany, but the airlines were booked to capacity. So Tom booked the 4:00 p.m. TWA flight 891 non-stop to Bonn, West Germany. He had to work on Donna's passports. He had taken some photos that were taken from the Massachusetts Department of Motor Vehicles that the DEA had confiscated. As he put together the first one, he paused for a moment and thanked Becky. Tom had hoped she wouldn't lose her job. He looked over at Donna sleeping, and realized how beautiful she was. Tom took a notepad and placed it on the little desk that was against the wall. He then glanced at his watch. It said 8:00 a.m., then he went to the bathroom. He then took a shower.

    Tom was coming out of the bathroom when Donna began to wake up. He told her that there was a notepad on the desk with her new name on it. He explained to her that she needed to practice writing her new signature. Tom wanted her to understand that it was very important, that her signature resembled all of her passports and documents. He was getting dressed when he was explaining to her what she needed to do. "Where are you going?" she asked. Tom was leaving to walk across the street to Sam's Diner to get some breakfast. He put on his sunglasses. Tom opened the door. The sun was shining on Donna's face. Tom looked back at her. He then smiled while he was closing the door. Donna got up from the bed. She saw the manila envelope on the desk. She emptied its contents. A gold wedding band fell out. She placed it on her finger. Donna then looked at the notepad, and she read her new name. It said Nancy McGonagall.

CHAPTER 10

An Investigation

Agents Kevin Crainey and Lisa Crosby had returned to Boston from Miami. It was Tuesday afternoon. The two agents were in Captain Donovan's office for a debriefing. Paul was chewing them out for their mess-up back in Miami, for letting Jonathan Loveday slip by their surveillance.

"What's Jonathan's condition?" Lisa asked.

"He's in the Intensive Care Unit at Mass General Hospital," replied Paul. The captain went on to inform Lisa and Kevin that Agent Allen's firearm was found at the Murphy residence. A round had been discharged. The bullet was retrieved from the wall next to a painting. Ballistics has confirmed that it belonged to Tom's weapon, and Donna's fingerprints were found all over the weapon. "At this time we haven't ruled out foul play with Tom's disappearance."

"Captain, has anyone gone over to Tom's house?" Kevin asked.

"I had local PD send a unit by, and they reported no unusual behavior at the Allen residence."

"So, Captain, what do you think happened to Tom?" Lisa asked.

"I'm not sure at this moment, and I won't know for sure until we can talk to Loveday."

Just as the captain had finished speaking, Lieutenant Stickles entered the office. "We just got a break. Massachusetts Bay Transit Authority Police have discovered Agent Allen's car parked at the

Greyhound bus station!" Captain Donovan ordered Agents Crosby and Crainey to the bus station.

Lisa and Kevin had jumped into their black Chevy Blazer. With the lights and sirens blaring, they raced to the bus station. Fifteen minutes later, they were about to pull into the parking lot. As the SUV was turning into the driveway, Lisa had to hit the brakes. Some pedestrians were walking across the sidewalk, where the driveway had connected to the street. She then proceeded to move the large SUV through some parked cars, then she sped to the end of the parking lot. Lisa could see two MBTA police units, with their blue lights flashing in the distance.

Kevin walked up to the parked Camaro. He looked through the driver's side window. He didn't notice anything unusual inside. Kevin then looked at the back glass hatch of the car, but the window was tinted, so he couldn't see through it. Kevin then pulled the door handle on the driver's side. The door was locked. Kevin then observed that the passenger's side inside lock knob was orange, which meant that the door was open. He then motioned to Lisa, who was on that side of the car, that the door was unlocked. Lisa then opened the door, and she looked inside the car.

Lisa told Kevin that she didn't see any blood inside the car, which meant that there was no physical evidence of a struggle or that a crime had been committed. She then pushed the automatic unlock button on the door panel so that Kevin could take a look inside the vehicle. Lisa opened the glove compartment. She had discovered Tom's badge, his keys, and wallet. She opened up the wallet. Lisa told Kevin that it was empty. She then pushed the button to unlock the back hatch. The hatch made a clicking sound, and Lisa knew it was unlocked, then she started to walk around to the back of the car. Just as she was about to lift the hatch, a flock of pigeons had taken to flight. Lisa had turned her head to observe them climbing into the blue sky. She then noticed a few seconds after the birds had flown away, the MBTA express train was speeding by. Lisa had turned her head to her right. She was watching the train as it passed by. A few seconds later it was gone. She was looking through the chain-link fence that was next to the car. The train tracks were at least twenty feet away. But Lisa had thought to herself that because of the noise that the train had made, it only seemed a few feet away when it sped by. Lisa continued to open the Camaro's back hatch. Kevin had walked to the back of the car. They both looked in; it was empty.

"What do you think this means, Kevin? Tom leaves his badge, keys, and an empty wallet."

"I don't know," replied Kevin.

"Let's go into the bus station to see if we can find some answers to these questions," Lisa said. The two agents proceeded to walk to the building entrance. As the two agents got closer to the door, Kevin and Lisa noticed some empty pints of vodka bottles lying on the ground. There were buses arriving and departing from the terminal in the foreground. Agent Crainey noticed how long the terminal was. He suggested to Lisa that they walk over to the ticket booth and ask some questions.

"Excuse me," said Lisa to the woman behind the counter. Lisa then proceeded to show her badge. "Have you seen this man?" Lisa then proceeded to show the woman a photograph of Tom.

"Lady, I see lots of people every day when I come to work, they all look alike to me!"

Agent Crosby then reached into her purse, then she pulled out a picture of Agent Allen when he was smiling. "How about this one?"

"Yes, I remember him. He was in here yesterday, I remember his dimples because he was flirting with me, he's so cute. I think he had purchased two tickets, maybe to Atlanta, let me check." The ticket booth clerk went to the back room to look at the purchase logs from the day before. A few moments later she returned.

"Here it is," she said. The clerk had the logbook in her hand. "What was his name?" she asked. "Thomas Allen," Lisa said. "He purchased two tickets to Atlanta Georgia at 9:45 p.m. for bus number 146 scheduled to leave the terminal at 11:00 p.m. However, bus number 146 was delayed several hours and didn't leave until 2:15 a.m. That bus was also scheduled for a four-hour layover in Baltimore, Maryland. Bus 146 is due to arrive in Atlanta Wednesday morning at 12:30." Agent Crainey was writing down all the information that the clerk had told them.

Agents Lisa Crosby and Kevin Crainey left the terminal. They were headed back to division headquarters.

Kevin and Lisa arrived back at headquarters. They were on their way to their office. They were riding up the elevator together. "Not one word," Lisa said. The elevator door had shut, and Kevin started to smile. "Why are you being so hostile?" Kevin asked. "You took advantage of me. Lisa, you wanted me, just as much as I wanted you." The elevator stopped, then the door opened. Lisa walked out first. She then turned her head. She looked at Kevin. Lisa then smiled at him. Kevin's eyes followed Lisa's movements. He began to watch her. Lisa was walking away. Kevin knew that she liked him.

The two agents were walking to the captain's office. They had some answers they knew would make Captain Donovan temporarily forget their mess-up in Miami. "Captain, we examined Tom's car. There was no evidence of foul play," Kevin said. Lisa had told Paul that Agent Allen purchased two tickets to Atlanta, Georgia. She was explaining to the captain that Tom and Donna could be on that bus and that it was due to arrive Wednesday morning. "Agent Allen either forced Ms. Murphy or she went willingly," Paul said. "I say she went willingly. I know that she had a crush on Tom, I put it in my report," Lisa said. "I read your report, Agent Crosby," the captain said.

Then Paul picked up the phone. He dialed the number for Atlanta Division. He wanted them to send some agents over to the Greyhound bus station. They were ordered to apprehend Agent Thomas Allen and Ms. Madonna Murphy when they arrived. Captain Donovan picked up the search warrant that was on his desk. He then handed it to Lisa and Kevin. Paul ordered them over to Agent Allen's residence to search the premises. Captain Donovan wanted to find as much evidence as possible for charges against his AWOL agent.

It was Tuesday evening, and Agents Crainey and Crosby were driving to Tom's residence. Agent Allen lived in the small town of Hanson, Massachusetts. It was about a thirty-five-minute ride from division headquarters. Lisa had decided that she wanted to take the Chevy Blazer to Tom's house. The two agents arrived at the house.

HE WAS ABOUT TO BETRAY HIS OATH

Lisa used Tom's key to enter the premises. She went in first. Both agents were being cautious as they entered. Lisa noticed Ozzy had run underneath the couch. Kevin went down the hallway toward the bedrooms. Lisa checked the garage and laundry room. The two agents found no sign of Tom, so they met each other back at the living room. Lisa then went over to where Ozzy had hidden. She called him. After a few minutes he came out from underneath the couch. She picked him up, and she started rubbing him underneath his neck.

"We can put him in the cat pound," Kevin said.

"Not while I'm still breathing." Lisa then went to laundry room. She put Ozzy into his traveling cage.

Lisa then proceeded to the kitchen, then she emptied the cat's litter box. She took it along with his dinner bowl and some food. Lisa then put Ozzy and his cat supplies in the truck. Kevin was searching the home. Lisa continued helping Kevin search. After an hour, they had realized that there was no incriminating evidence that they could find. The agents had decided to call it a night. Lisa dropped Kevin off at the division. She then took the Blazer home so she could remove Ozzy from her vehicle.

Kevin went up to the office. He wanted to complete some of his paperwork. It was a long day. Agent Crainey had traveled a lot of miles in the air and on the ground. Kevin began to ponder how Jonathan Loveday slipped by him. He knew that he was a top-notch agent. Agent Kevin Crainey realized that he was falling for Lisa. She was the type of woman that was his equal. Kevin had many women before. But none of them compared to Agent Lisa Crosby. Kevin looked at his watch. It said 9:20 p.m. He had decided to call it a night. He was leaving the precinct. He decided to stop by Lieutenant Stickles's office. The lieutenant was sitting at his desk. Kevin asked the lieutenant, "What's the condition of Jonathan Loveday?"

"Kevin, he's comatose."

It was now Wednesday morning. Kevin had a sleepless night. He just could not believe that his friend and former partner would betray the oath that he had sworn to the agency. Kevin and Tom had gone through a lot together over the years as agent partners. If anyone had known agent Allen, it was Kevin Crainey. He had woken up several times during the night. His intuition was telling him that there had to be something more than the love for a woman. Kevin got out of the bed at 5:30 a.m. He went to the bathroom. He then looked into the mirror. He stared at himself for a brief moment and turned on the cold-water handle. The water started to run into the sink. Kevin put some in his hands, then he splashed his face. He then stared back into the mirror, and with an angry voice, he yelled, "I will get to the bottom of this, if it's the last thing that I ever do!" He walked out of his bathroom. He started walking toward his kitchen. Just then, Kevin had decided to give Lisa a call. He was about to pick up his telephone when it started to ring. Kevin answered it. It was Captain Donovan. The two men talked for a few minutes, then Kevin hung up the phone. He then phoned Lisa, and he told her that he was coming by to pick her up.

Agent Crainey had taken the Ford LTD Crown Victoria home last night. He had told Lisa that he would be by her house around 8:00 a.m. Kevin arrived at her neighborhood a little bit past eight. Agent Lisa Crosby lived in one of those types of neighborhoods where all the houses looked identical. Kevin had been to her home one other time previously with Tom, so he had an idea where she had lived. But as he drove around through the neighborhood, the only way that he had recognized her house was that he spotted the black Chevrolet Blazer parked in her driveway.

Kevin pulled up to the house. Lisa was standing outside waiting. "Good morning," Kevin said. Lisa just got into the car. They drove off, then both agents started to talk about how they had a sleepless night. Kevin and Lisa both worked with Agent Allen, so they knew his method of operation. "Where are we going?" Lisa asked. "The Murphy residence, we need to take a look around!"

Kevin drove to the expressway. He then drove onto the ramp, and that's when he looked up at the green expressway sign. It said, "Carver–Plympton, 37 miles."

While the two agents were driving, Kevin had told Lisa that the captain had called him earlier this morning. Kevin had informed

Agent Crosby that Tom was now officially considered a fugitive. And Donna most likely went with Tom by her own free will. Kevin explained to Lisa that the agents in Atlanta had boarded the number 146 Greyhound bus. Tom and Donna were nowhere to be found. Instead, the agents had apprehended Lorenzo the panhandler. Lorenzo told the agents that Tom had given him the ticket. Donna seemed like she was happy to be with Tom. "I bet she was," Lisa said. Kevin had ignored Lisa's remark. He continued to tell her what Lorenzo said, that they both had suitcases.

The sun was shining very brightly through the front windshield of their car. It was reflecting on Lisa. Her blond hair started to radiate from the luminous rays. Kevin had looked over at her. He then realized just how pretty Lisa was.

They arrived at Donna's house. Kevin pulled into the driveway. It had snowed about an inch or two last night in the Carver area. "Well, at least we know that no one else has been here," Lisa said.

The two agents made fresh tracks through the snow as they walked up to the front door. Kevin pulled away the yellow crime scene tape. It was taped across the front of the doorway. He then broke the police seal. Agent Crainey was the first one to enter the home. Lisa had followed him. "There is quite a bit of blood on the floor," Lisa said. The two agents had looked at the broken glass pieces that were scattered across the floor. "There was a real struggle here," Kevin said. Agent Crosby told Kevin that she would follow the blood trail upstairs. Agent Crainey went to the kitchen area. Lisa started climbing the stairs. When she arrived at the top, she stopped for a second to look around. It was a little dark, so she shined her flashlight against the wall. Lisa saw the light switch and turned it on. She could see the trail of blood drops leading down the hallway, so she followed the trail. It had led her into a bedroom. "So this is her bedroom," she mumbled. Lisa looked into the bathroom because the light was left on. She then looked at the bed. Lisa walked into the bathroom. When she entered, she saw herself in the giant mirror along the wall. Lisa then glanced at the shower because the door was left open. Lisa then looked in the sink cabinets. She didn't see or notice anything that shouldn't belong there.

Lisa turned around, and she walked out of the bathroom. She then proceeded to walk to the closet. While she was inside the closet, she noticed how big it was. Donna had one of those types of closet that you could move around in. Lisa was glancing at Donna's many pairs of shoes. "Just what in the hell am I looking for?" she mumbled. Meanwhile, Kevin had opened the basement door. He was walking down the steep steps. He reached the bottom, and he noticed that the team that had executed the search warrant had left the place a mess. There were boxes thrown all around. Kevin turned on his flashlight. He then started to scan the room. He walked toward the back of the cellar. Kevin shined the light onto the wall. He started to turn around when he noticed something strange about it. Kevin had looked at the bottom of the wall. He saw a little lever protruding, so he pulled it, and the wall opened up slightly. "What do we have here?" he said.

Lisa had walked out of the closet. She looked at the bed. She saw the bloodstained pillow that Jonathan had laid his head on. She turned and looked at the fireplace. She decided walk over to get a better look at the mantel. "There is something missing," she said. Lisa looked at the several picture frames. She had noticed that one picture was missing. There was a space that didn't have dust on it.

She took the chair that was sitting at the desk and brought it over to the fireplace. Lisa climbed onto the chair so she could get a better look on top of the mantel. "Look what we have here," she said. Agent Lisa Crosby had just found the single piece of evidence that told her that Donna Murphy went willingly with Tom. Lisa knew that the picture that Donna had taken from the mantel was very sentimental to her. Donna had placed there her diamond engagement ring, the one that was given to her by Jonathan Loveday.

Agents Crainey and Crosby left the Murphy residence. They were on their way back to Boston. While they we're traveling, they started to discuss what evidence they had found. This evidence was relevant to why Agent Allen had left the agency. "Tom buys two tickets to Atlanta, Georgia. He then sends Lorenzo there," Kevin said. "That was deliberately done to buy him some time," Lisa said. Suddenly, Kevin had to change lanes a semitrailer truck moved into his lane. "Donna takes a photo that was important to her, so there was nothing irrelevant found at Tom's house," Kevin said. "It just doesn't make any sense," replied Lisa. Kevin again changed lanes to the fast lane. The car accelerated a little faster. Agent Kevin Crainey wanted to get back to the precinct.

They arrived at the division. Kevin had dropped off Lisa at the front of the building. He had driven around to the parking garage. It was located in the back of the building. Agent Crosby walked through the front entrance. She went through the metal detector. "Good afternoon, Ralph." Lisa was retrieving her badge and firearm from the conveyer belt. Lisa had turned around to walk down the corridor toward the elevator. She hesitated for a brief moment. She then began to stare at the wall where the portrait of the agency director and the president hung. Lisa turned around, and she asked Ralph, "When did they replace President Reagan's portrait with President Bush's?"

"That was done a few weeks ago, Agent Crosby."

Lisa was sitting at her desk completing some of her much-needed reports that she was behind on; there was a lot of paperwork. She would glance up every now and then at Tom's desk, then she would continue to type and write.

Kevin had walked across the street to the food vendor. He bought some hot dogs for himself and Lisa. Kevin knew that Lisa liked hot dogs because they had eaten a lot of them during their stakeout at Loveday's house in Miami.

"I bought you some lunch." Kevin had walked up to Lisa. He had placed the bag of food he was carrying on her desk. She opened the bag. She placed the hot dog on her desk and removed the tin foil. "Kevin, you read my mind. I was just sitting here thinking how hungry I was." She opened up a mustard packet and squeezed some on her hot dog. Kevin sat down at Tom's desk. He opened up his bag, and he joined Lisa for lunch. The two of them stared at each other as they ate. Kevin had looked up at the clock on the wall. It said 12:15 p.m. About twenty minutes later, Captain Paul Donovan was screaming for Lisa and Kevin to get in his office. "Doesn't he ever stop yelling?"

Lisa said. The two agents walked into the office. The captain went on to explain that he had just received the agency phone records for Agent Allen's home and office phones. "It seems that Tom made a call to the FBI. He spoke with an agent from the Philadelphia division. Agent Allen talked for about twenty-five minutes with an agent by the name of Brian Singer. I want you to follow up on their conversation." The captain dismissed Kevin and Lisa.

The two agents left the captain's office. They went back to their desks. Kevin picked up Tom's phone. He was dialing the Philadelphia division. "Federal Bureau of Investigation, Janet speaking. How may I direct your call?"

"This is Agent Kevin Crainey of the Drug Enforcement Agency, Boston Division. Identification number 10014326."

"Yes, Agent Crainey, how may I direct your call?"

"I need to speak with Special Agent Brian Singer."

"Please hold, Agent Crainey, while I transfer your call."

"Hello, Agent Crainey, Brian speaking. What can I do for you?"

Kevin explained to Brian that he was Tom's partner, that he and Tom were working on a case, and that Tom had since disappeared. Kevin had told Brian that he suspected some foul play. He then asked Brian if he could recall the conversation that he had with Tom a few days ago. Special Agent Singer told Kevin that he did remember his conversation with Agent Thomas Allen. Then he told Agent Crainey to hold on. Brian went to retrieve the file.

"Kevin, I am going to the soda machine to get a Pepsi. Do you want anything?"

"Yes, Lisa, grab me a Sprite!" While Lisa was walking away, Kevin started to stare at her again. Kevin was starting to see Lisa more as a girlfriend than a partner. His feelings for her were growing stronger, and he knew that she liked him.

Special Agent Brian Singer explained to Kevin what he and Tom had discussed on Monday. Brian told Kevin that Tom wanted him to search for information on a gentleman by the name of Wilhelm Strausvon. Brian then read to Kevin his file. "Wilhelm Strausvon arrived in the United States aboard a navy supply ship, along with two German officers and two German physicists. Wilhelm was a major general for the Luftwaffe. He also was a medical doctor. He arrived here on August 18, 1945, at the Weymouth Naval Base in Massachusetts. Wilhelm was given top military clearance from the Allied War Department. His name was changed to William Shultz. That's where his file ends. There is no more information on Mr. Shultz. It seems as if he has vanished from the face of the earth."

Kevin thanked Agent Singer for his help. Kevin hung up the phone. Lisa was returning from the soda machine. She placed Kevin's Sprite on Tom's desk.

"Well?" Lisa said. Kevin went on to explain to her what Special Agent Singer had told him. Kevin mentioned the names Wilhelm Strausvon and William Shultz. Lisa didn't recognize either name. Kevin then looked at the clock. It said 1:15 p.m.

Agents Crosby and Crainey were conversing back and forth with each other. They both agreed that Tom would not have jeopardized his career over a woman. They both knew their friend and colleague. There had to be another reason for his irrational behavior. Kevin had come to the conclusion that whatever it was, it involved Wilhelm Strausvon, a.k.a. William Shultz. "We need to find this person," Lisa said. It was getting late; Kevin and Lisa were frustrated. They had decided to call it a day.

Kevin drove Lisa back to her house. The two were sitting in the car talking. "You want to come in for a drink?" Kevin accepted her offer. The two agents walked into the house. When the door opened, Ozzy scrambled into his traveling cage. Lisa had left it set up on the floor for him to sleep in it. He wasn't used to being at her house. She had thought that the cat would be more comfortable with something that was more familiar to him. Lisa walked behind the bar, and she asked Kevin what he wanted to drink. "I'll have a scotch." Kevin sat down on the couch. Lisa walked over to him, then she gave him his glass of whisky. "Thank you," Kevin said. Kevin gave Lisa a wink with his left eye.

Lisa had told Kevin that she was going to slip into something more comfortable. She had left the room. Kevin was drinking his whisky. He started looking around the living room at the various items that Lisa owned. That's when he noticed the cat sitting in his cage. Kevin got up from the couch. He then walked over to the cat's cage. He reached in and grabbed Ozzy. He started to pet him, and he told him what a good kitty he was. Kevin then set him down. Ozzy ran away. Kevin noticed when he picked Ozzy up his claws had stuck to the blanket. The cat had pulled some of it out of his cage. He reached his hand inside the cage. He pulled out the rest of the blanket that the cat had slept on. "Well, look what we have here." Kevin picked up the black book that resembled a thin softcover New Testament Bible. The book had fallen out of the cat's cage. Kevin then went back to the couch. He sat down and started to read it. Kevin could not believe what his eyes were reading. There it was, the single piece of evidence that had eluded him and Lisa all day. Kevin yelled for Lisa. She came running out of her bedroom. She asked Kevin what was wrong. "I know who Wilhelm Strausvon is. His name is Richard Rittenberg."

"Oh my God! He's a patient at Woodridge Nursing Home," Lisa yelled. Kevin had suggested that tomorrow they'd go pay Mr. Rittenberg a visit. Lisa had told Kevin that Richard had a stroke; he could barely speak. "We will see about that. There are some pages missing from this book. We need to know what they are," Agent Kevin Crainey said.

It was Thursday morning. Agents Crainey and Crosby were in Captain Donovan's office. They had asked the captain for a search warrant to search Mr. Rittenberg's room at the nursing home. They wanted to question him about the diary and the contents of the missing pages. But Captain Donovan didn't think that was a good idea. He was concerned about the media getting ahold of this story. Captain Donovan explained to his agents that the Justice Department wanted this matter to stay internal. Captain Donovan told Lisa and Kevin to see if they could convince Michelle Bettes if she would allow them to question Mr. Rittenberg.

It was a cold day. Lisa had asked Kevin if he would turn the heat up. They were driving the Chevy Blazer, and the big SUV took a while to heat up. The day was cloudy. It looked as if it was going to snow. Kevin and Lisa arrived at the nursing home, and they went straight to Michelle's office. "Let me do the talking," Lisa said. She wanted Kevin to keep quiet. They walked through the door, and Michelle was sitting at her desk. "Good morning, Michelle," Lisa said. Lisa told Michelle her dilemma, but Michelle was not about to break protocol and risk a lawsuit. She was upset at Lisa for deceiving her, also for Lisa's deception for hiring her. Michelle went on to tell Lisa that Mr. Rittenberg was awarded to their care by a trustee for the estate of the deceased Mr. Albert Bonheoffer. That was all the information that she would divulge, unless Lisa had a search warrant. Mrs. Bettes had told the two agents to leave.

Kevin and Lisa were leaving Michelle's office when an announcement had come over the intercom. "Code yellow, room 321." Michelle practically had pushed Lisa out of her way to respond to the emergency. Lisa told Kevin that this might be their only chance to talk to Mr. Rittenberg. The two agents walked toward his room. They climbed the flight of stairs and hurried to his room. They had to walk past the nurses' station. "Hello, Laura," Nurse Kelly said. So as not to arouse suspicion, Lisa stopped, and she talked to Kelly. She then introduced Kevin as her boyfriend. She was explaining to Kelly that she needed to see Mr. Rittenberg. Lisa and Kevin left. They walked to room 218. They walked inside. Richard looked up. He saw Laura. Richard recognized her. He then smiled.

"Hello, Mr. Rittenberg." Lisa tucked his pillow under his head. She started to explain to him why Donna had not been in to see him. She then reassured him that his secret would remain a secret and that no one would ever know about his past. Kevin had walked over to the closet. He was going through his personal items. Lisa said to Richard that the person who took Donna tore out some pages in his diary. She needed to know what they were so she could find Donna.

Lisa then showed Richard the book. He had a worried look on his face. Lisa again reassured him that no one knew about the book. He seemed to calm down a bit. "Richard, do you remember what the torn pages were about?" He turned his head. He started to struggle to say the word. "Cold," Lisa had repeated the word, but Richard was getting frustrated. About that time, Kevin had come over to the bed.

He then put his hand on the bed rail. Richard looked at Kevin's large navy ring on his finger, and he said the word "cold." Kevin had followed his eyes. He had noticed that Richard was looking at his ring. "Gold, Mr. Rittenberg." Suddenly, Richard smiled. Lisa wanted to know where, so she said, "Germany!" Richard smiled again. Lisa and Kevin started to talk to each other. They began to ask Richard more questions concerning the gold. Kevin could sense that Richard had known where it was. But the more questions Kevin asked, the more agitated Richard had become. Suddenly, one of his monitors started to beep. Lisa knew it was his respirator, and soon there would be a code yellow. She needed to act very quickly. Lisa said the name Ingrid Kaufmann. Then she looked into Richard's eyes. They told her that Ingrid was the person that she needed to find.

The two agents got into their vehicle and left the nursing home. They were on their way back to Boston. They started again to converse with each other. Lisa had opened the journal. She had noticed that there were many log entries that had pointed to the German city of Nuremberg. "Kevin, there was a clinic where Ingrid worked. I think that's the next place we should look." Kevin agreed with his partner. "Now, I know why Tom did what he had done," Kevin said. Lisa and Kevin had realized that Agent Thomas Allen would definitely have risked his career for a large amount of gold. They both looked at each other and smiled. They had decided to make a pact with each other to find the gold themselves. But first they needed to find Tom and Donna. Germany was a large country; being divided after the war, it might take some time. The two agents realized that they needed to leave as soon as possible. Tom and Donna already had a few days' head start.

"Lisa, let's not mention this to the captain, about anything concerning the gold."

"Okay," she said. Agents Kevin Crainey and Lisa Crosby had ambitions of their own; they both looked at each other and smiled.

Agents Kevin Crainey and Lisa Crosby arrived at division headquarters. They were in Captain Paul Donovan's office. Lisa had informed Paul about their latest lead on the whereabouts of Agent

HE WAS ABOUT TO BETRAY HIS OATH

Thomas Allen and suspect Donna Murphy. Paul quickly reminded his two trustworthy agents about the rules of engagement. The agency director did not want the West German officials involved in this internal agency matter. Captain Donovan told Lisa and Kevin that they would have to travel as a married couple, not as agents. Paul also insisted that when they apprehend Agent Allen and Ms. Murphy, they were to bring them to the US Embassy in Bonn.

It was Saturday afternoon. Agents Kevin and Lisa Crainey had boarded Pan Am flight 760. The two agents were on their way to Bonn, West Germany. They had just taken off from Logan International Airport. The captain of the airplane had just suspended flight restrictions. Lisa looked at her hand. She was admiring her wedding band.

Lisa then looked at Kevin. "Don't you get any ideas about consummating our marriage."

Kevin turned his head, and he looked at her. "We'd already done that in Miami." Lisa then punched him in the shoulder, and she giggled. "Lisa, who's taking care of Ozzy?"

"My sister Linda."

Just then a stewardess had arrived with her refreshment cart, and she asked Lisa if she wanted anything. Lisa was sitting on the outside of the row of seats. She then told the woman that she wanted the ham-and-cheese sandwich and a Pepsi. The airline stewardess then bent a little toward Kevin. He was staring at her chest. Kevin then noticed her name tag; it said Heather. "Sir, would you like something?"

"Yes, ma'am, I'll have a Sprite."

Kevin and Lisa were discussing their strategy, of what they needed to do when they reached West Germany. They had hoped Ingrid was still alive; she would be in her early eighties. They talked for a little while. Lisa then wanted to take a nap. Kevin had decided that he was going to watch the movie that was playing on the big screen; it was *Ferris Bueller's Day Off.*

The plane had landed at the airport. Lisa and Kevin went through customs. Their passports had checked out. The West German customs agents allowed them to continue on their way. They walked outside the airport terminal. It was a cold night out. Kevin hailed a Taxi. "Where to?" the driver asked. Kevin put their luggage in the trunk. He then told the driver to drive to the Hilton Hotel.

The taxi pulled up to the hotel entrance. Two bellboys quickly came over to the taxi. They carried Kevin and Lisa's luggage. Kevin tipped the taxi driver. The couple went into the hotel. They walked up to the clerk. "May I help you?"
Kevin looked at the man and he told him that he had a room reserved for Mr. and Mrs. Kevin Crainey.
"Yes, Mr. and Mrs. Crainey, your room is 218." The clerk was handing Kevin the key when Kevin and Lisa both looked at each other and simultaneously said, "Mr. Rittenberg!"
"This has to be a good omen," Kevin said. Kevin and Lisa both started laughing while they continued walking to the elevators. The clerk rang his bell, and two bellboys came over to the counter, and they carried the Craineys' luggage. Lisa had commented to Kevin on how beautiful the hotel was. She had liked the many freshly cut flowers that were laid out in vases on the tables. Being winter, it made the hotel lobby smell like spring.

Kevin and Lisa both woke up Sunday late in the afternoon. They were feeling the effects of the time zone change and jet lag. They had showered and ate some breakfast. "Hurry up, Lisa. We need to get going." Lisa was in the bathroom getting herself ready when she came out. Kevin had complimented her on how beautiful she looked.
They took a taxi to the US Embassy. The two agents walked into the consulate. They told the marine sergeant that they had an appointment with Ambassador Paul Hunt. A few moments later they met with the ambassador. Paul reminded Kevin and Lisa that they did not have diplomatic immunity. They needed to stay within the rules of engagement. The three of them shook hands. The US ambassador had invited them to dinner later that evening.

The sergeant then took them to the embassy armory, and he issued them standard firearms. The two agents got back into the taxi, which had waited for them to return. Then the driver proceeded to drive them to a car rental dealership. They rented a blue four-door sedan. Agents Kevin and Lisa Crainey drove back to the Hilton Hotel.

Kevin and Lisa arrived back at the hotel. They went upstairs to their room. Their room was a large room. It had a full bath and a large outside balcony. Lisa sat down on the couch, then she started to read Richard's journal. The more she read about Ingrid, the more she wanted to meet her. Lisa had become intrigued by what was written about her. "Lisa, you need to get ready. The ambassador is sending over a limousine to pick us up." Lisa closed the book, and she looked at her wedding band. She also was wearing Donna's engagement ring.

CHAPTER 11

The Getaway

It was another cold day in West Germany. Agents Kevin and Lisa Crainey had gotten up early. They were very eager to meet Ingrid. Kevin was still a little hungover from the previous night. He and the ambassador really had a good time. They both found out that they had a lot in common. Lisa had gotten along well with Paul's wife even though she would sometimes give her dirty looks because her husband would not stop staring and flirting with her. Lisa was an attractive woman. She knew how to handle those types of men. Lisa had to politely remind the ambassador several times that he was married. The two agents quietly checked out of the Hilton, and they were soon driving on the expressway. They were headed to the city of Nuremberg.

Several hours later, Lisa and Kevin arrived at the city of Nuremberg. It was a large city, and by reading the journal, they had a rough idea of where the clinic was located. They had driven to the northern outskirts of the city, then Lisa had suggested that they stop at a gas station to ask someone there for directions. Lisa filled up the gas tank while Kevin went inside. "Excuse me, sir, do you know where I could find a health-care facility around here?"

"Yes, sir. There is the Ingrid Kaufmann Memorial Hospital about seven miles down the road."

Kevin thanked the man, then he paid him for the gas. He then went back to his car.

"So, Kevin, what did he say?"

"You won't believe this, Lisa, but Ingrid has her own hospital. It's named after her!" Lisa looked at Kevin, then she smiled at him. Kevin began to tell her more about Ingrid's hospital. Kevin and Lisa drove down the street toward the direction of the hospital. They drove into the parking lot and parked their vehicle, and they both went inside. When they entered into the facility, Lisa noticed a plaque that hung on the wall with an engraved image of Ingrid. Lisa looked a little further down the corridor just before the patients' waiting room. She had seen a custodian sweeping the floor. Lisa approached the man. She then started to explain to him that Ingrid was her lost grandmother, that she had just recently found out about that, and that she had traveled all the way from the United States. Lisa continued to explain to the man that she needed to find out if Ingrid was still alive.

The custodian told Lisa that Ms. Kaufmann was in fact still alive. The last that he had heard was that she was in a rest home in Hannover. The man did not know the name of the rest home. Lisa gave him a hug and kiss on his cheek. Kevin shook the man's hand. He then thanked him. The two agents quickly left the hospital. They returned to their car. Kevin and Lisa knew that they had their work cut out for them. Hannover was a large city. They would have to find a rest home and check every name at that facility in order to find the woman who might hold the key to where Hermann Goering's gold is. This will also ultimately lead them to Agent Thomas Allen and suspect Madonna Murphy.

It was the second week in the month of April. Spring had arrived early in West Germany. Jim and Nancy McGonagall had bought a nice little ranch house. They had settled in a small town just outside of the city of Hannover. Jim had wanted a place to live where he would not be surrounded by a lot of houses. So he found a home that was located on a golf course. Jim had a neighbor who lived to the right side of him. His house was at least sixty yards away from Jim's house. His other neighbor to the left of him was at least forty yards away from his house. There were only a few more homes located on the private road. His neighbors to the left of him were an older couple in their sixties; their names were Scott and Cheryl Laiweneek. They were originally from the United States, but they had decided to retire in West Germany. Scott had been an enlisted man for the US Air Force. He had held the rank of chief master sergeant. Jim had to be very careful around Scott. He did not want Scott to suspect that he had any military training. Cheryl and Nancy had gotten along very well. Cheryl treated Nancy like she was her very own daughter. Jim had told the Laiweneeks that he had inherited his late father's fortune. He and Nancy wanted to get far away from his greedy family members. So they too had decided to leave the States.

Jim had purchased a new 4 × 4 extended cab flat-bed pickup truck. He had wanted something powerful enough to pull the twenty-eight-foot boat that he was about to buy. He had found the lake a month ago. Now that the weather was getting warm, Jim knew that the ice would almost be melted. Jim also had bought a used van that he had parked in his garage. His garage was separate from the house, so he had to walk about fifty feet to reach it. Jim was doing a lot of work on the engine. He put in heavy-duty shocks and new brakes. He also put in new power steering and rebuilt his transmission. Jim had done a lot of minor improvements to his van; he knew that he needed a vehicle capable of carrying heavy loads.

Nancy was sitting on her couch watching television. She had found a store in Hannover that sold classic American movie videos. She put in the VCR an old Katharine Hepburn movie; *Without Love* was the name. While she was watching the movie, she had noticed that the actor Spencer Tracy looked like her father when she was a child. She then paused the movie for a few moments. Nancy went to her bedroom dresser; she then picked up the picture of her father. Nancy began to stare at it; she then began to shed some tears Nancy had missed him dearly, and she was remembering the day when she was six when Richard had asked her if he could call her Donna.

Kevin and Lisa had settled in Hannover. They had rented a nice two-bedroom apartment on Hagenstrasse Road. It was a dead-end street. Their three-story house was at the end, right near the train tracks. When the train would pass by the house, it would vibrate and shake, but Lisa liked where they had lived. They moved on the second floor. Lisa also fell in love with city of Hannover. She admired the historical section of the city. It had many medieval features, including its buildings and narrow streets. There were many fourteenth-century Catholic churches well preserved, along with its museums and landscaped gardens.

It was late April. Kevin and Lisa searched over twenty nursing rest homes. There were a few rest homes left on their list. Kevin and Lisa desperately wanted to find and speak with Ingrid. They had driven into a new rest home that was recently built. Lisa had walked through the entrance door. She walked up to the counter and asked the nurse if there was a resident by the name of Ingrid Kaufmann.

"Yes, there is. May I ask who is inquiring?"

"My name is Lisa, and I am her granddaughter from the United States."

The nurse gave them directions to Ingrid's room, but when they got there, she wasn't there. There was a nurse walking down the hallway. "Excuse me, have you seen Ingrid Kaufmann?" Lisa asked. The nurse had told Lisa that Ms. Kaufmann was sitting outside on the patio taking in the fresh spring air.

Kevin and Lisa walked up to Ingrid. She was reading a novel. Lisa had commented to Kevin how beautiful she was, but Kevin didn't think so. Lisa hit him, and she told him to be quiet, to let her do the talking. Ingrid looked up, and she saw the couple staring at her. "Do I know you?" Lisa responded to her question with a no. She then quickly introduced herself and her husband, Kevin. Ingrid then closed her book. She then wanted to know what they wanted. "Ms. Kaufmann, we have traveled here from the United States to see you."

"That, my dear, is a long way to travel," Ingrid said.

"My father, Wilhelm Strausvon, wanted me to find you."

Ingrid's face had changed demeanor. Her eyes were wide open. "How is he?" Ingrid asked. Lisa then went on to explain to Ingrid what had happen to Wilhelm. She continued to tell her about his life after he had left Germany.

Ingrid had asked Lisa if Wilhelm had married her mother. Lisa had told her no. Ingrid then started to shed a tear. "Why are you crying?" Ingrid went on to explain to Lisa that she and her father were lovers and that he had promised her before he had left Germany. "Wilhelm said that he would never get married. He had loved his wife, Marlene, and after her death, he was a broken man." She told Lisa that they had remained lovers until the day that he left her. He boarded the train to France. Kevin began to poke Lisa in her back. He wanted her to ask Ingrid if she knew about the gold. Lisa turned around, and she said, "Be patient, Kevin." Ingrid and Lisa continued to converse with each other about Wilhelm. Lisa pulled up a chair, and she sat down. Soon Ingrid Kaufmann was getting comfortable talking with Lisa. "You know, I used to have blond hair just like you when I was your age," Ingrid said. Lisa had smiled, then Ingrid told Lisa how pretty she was.

Jim had purchased his boat, a sonar meter, and some underwater diving apparatuses. Jim and Nancy had loaded up their gear. They were finally ready to go and search for Hermann Goering's lost gold. They were very excited about the prospect of treasure hunting. Nancy was making sandwiches for their lunch. She went to the sliding glass back door. She tried to slide the door open, but it was hard for her because she had a knife in one of her hands. Nancy also was carrying a loaf of bread in her other hand. So she went over to the table that was against the wall. Nancy set the knife on it next to a vase full of freshly cut flowers. She finally got the door opened, and she asked Jim how many sandwiches he wanted. Jim had asked Nancy to help him. He wanted her to check if the brake and direction signals were working correctly on the boat. Jim started to mash the brake pedal inside the truck. Nancy told him everything was working just fine. Jim loaded up his truck with his equipment he had in his van. They packed their lunches, and they were on their way.

Jim and Nancy McGonagall arrived at the lake. Jim drove down the dirt road until he reached the end. There was another truck parked to Jim's right. He drove carefully by so he would not hit its boat trailer. The road was narrow. Nancy said she couldn't see their boat on the lake. Jim had reminded her that it was a large body of water and that they were probably fishing on the other side. He then backed his boat into the lake Nancy held the rope while Jim parked their truck. Jim held on to the boat while Nancy climbed in; he then pushed them out into deeper water. Jim climbed in. He started the boat's engine, backed up a bit, and turned the boat around. They then headed for deeper water. After about fifty yards or so, he slowed the boat down. He then dropped into the water the sonar meter listening device. It sends out sound waves that emit ultrasonic pulses using its submerged sensitive microphone. This registers water depth and large objects on the lake bottom. Jim knew that he needed to head out about one hundred yards. According to the ripped pages he had torn from Richard's journal, that's where the gold should be. He was about 125 yards out when the monitor had started to beep. The yellow lights began to flash. Jim McGonagall was in fifty feet of water.

"What is it?" Nancy asked. Jim told her he couldn't tell; he had to go down and take a look, so he let down the anchor. He then put on his diving gear. Nancy had a worried look on her face, but Jim reassured her that his days in the navy had trained him for underwater demolitions. "I'll be back in a flash." Jim fell over the side and into the water. Nancy looked over the side of the boat; all she could see was air bubbles rising to the surface. She did not budge the whole time that Jim was gone. About fifteen minutes later, Jim had returned to the surface. He was climbing onto the boat, then Nancy asked him what it was. "It was an old World War II American P-51 Mustang fighter plane, and the pilot was still entombed in the cockpit. God rest his soul!"

Jim quickly pulled up the anchor, so he then decided to troll in the direction heading east. The couple started to eat their sandwiches, and they drank some water. It was pretty warm out; the sun was shining. It was at least seventy-five degrees. "Jim, do you think we will find the gold?"

"Nancy, if what I have read about Hermann Goering is true, he stole a lot of art and gold from the countries that the Nazis had occupied during the Second World War!"

Suddenly, the light on the monitor started to flash again. "Nancy, there's something here." Jim let down the anchor; it rested sixty feet to the bottom. Jim put his breathing tank on his back and put his snorkel in his mouth and his watertight goggle mask on his face. He then looked at Nancy. He leaned over the side of the boat. Jim fell into the water. Nancy rushed over to where he went in; all she could see again was air bubbles rising to the surface. "Be careful, honey," Nancy said. Jim turned on his flashlight, and he swam to the bottom of the lake. He soon discovered that it was covered with some large dead tree trunks. Jim shined his flashlight to his right when suddenly out of the dark murky water a large-mouth bass swam directly toward him; it had startled Jim a bit. The bass was at least a thirty pounder, and the fish quickly swam off to the left of Jim. Just as quickly as it appeared, the fish vanished in the murky water. Jim had decided to swim in the direction that the large fish went. He saw something in the distance protruding out from behind a huge dead tree stump. Jim McGonagall flashed his light on the tree the closer he had swam. He noticed a black object protruding. "This isn't a log," he said. Jim McGonagall could not believe what his eyes were seeing. There it was, just like the German Reich Marshal had told Richard: a brass chest the size of a coffin.

Jim's heart had begun to beat real fast. He pulled out his bolt cutter. He then cut off the padlock that was on the chest. He paused for a second, then he stared at the chest, then he slowly opened it. The water became radiant. There was a bright yellow glow. Jim looked at all of that gold. "I'm rich," he said to himself. He looked at his watch and quickly closed the cover. He needed to get back to the surface. He was about to run out of oxygen. Jim tied a heavy-duty fishing line to the handle on the chest. He then swam back to the boat. Nancy had not taken her eyes off the water since Jim had gone in twenty minutes ago. She saw the bubbles start to rise to the surface. She knew that he was returning. "I found it!" Jim had screamed as he climbed onto the boat. Jim opened up his hand. He had some of the most precious gold coins that Nancy had ever seen. She screamed; they then both hugged and kissed each other. Then Jim quickly tied the fishing line to an extra-large-size fishing bobber. He then placed the bobber on the water to help him mark where the gold was. Jim then changed air tanks, took several large heavy-duty cloth bags, and then went back into the water to retrieve their gold.

Kevin and Lisa left the rest home. They had gotten the information that they wanted. Ingrid had known about the gold, but she never said a word to anyone. She promised the man that she loved that she would remain silent. Ingrid had thought that Wilhelm would someday come back for her and the treasure. Kevin and Lisa were driving toward the lake; they were not interested in Tom and Donna anymore. They had decided that they wanted to get rich. They also thought about perhaps even really getting married. Kevin and Lisa both had found that they had a lot in common. The two had become lovers as well as partners.

Soon they had arrived at the lake.. Kevin drove past the water tower. He then drove down the dirt road. Just before he reached the end, he saw two trucks parked. Kevin drove slowly past the first truck, then he passed the black 4 × 4 flatbed. He pulled his car into the clearing, and he stopped; he then backed up a little bit. "Well, what do we have here?" Kevin said. Lisa and Kevin got out of their vehicle. They walked up to the clearing. The two agents noticed a boat about seventy-five yards out. Kevin took out his binoculars. He then proceeded to scan the boat. "Lisa, you won't believe this. Donna is on that boat!"

"Give me those binoculars." Kevin passed them to Lisa. She then looked at the boat. "It looks like someone is coming out of the water, it's Tom!" Lisa passed the binoculars back to Kevin. The two DEA agents quickly realized that Tom and Donna had found their gold. All they had to do was sit back and wait for their opportunity to take what they believed had belonged to them. Kevin walked over to the first truck. He looked through the window. He then walked over to the black flatbed, and he did the same. Kevin went back to his car. He opened his trunk, then Kevin took out a small tracking device.

He then walked back to the flatbed. Agent Kevin Crainey reached under the truck near the gas tank. He then placed the device. Kevin and Lisa then drove about a quarter of a mile away from the lake, and they parked. "Kevin, how did you know that the black truck was Tom's?"

"That's an easy answer, Lisa. There were Ozzy Osbourne cassettes tapes scattered all over the seat!" Then Lisa looked at Kevin, and she started to laugh. "I knew it was a good omen when our hotel room number was 218," she said. Kevin looked at her, and he too started laughing. "Yes, Lisa, it's like taking candy from a baby," he said.

Jim and Nancy had returned to the shore. Jim had put the boat back onto the trailer. He had transferred the gold to the back of their truck. Some of the cloth bags were heavy. They had contained gold bars, while some of the other bags had coins. Jim covered the back of the truck with a tan canvas. They both were really happy to leave the lake. Jim and Nancy had retrieved Hermann Goering's gold. As they drove away from the lake, they began to sing. "We're in the money." They both were very jubilant as they laughed and sang. The McGonagalls arrived home. The sun had started to set. Jim backed up the trailer. He disconnected the boat from the truck. Nancy had gone into the house to start cooking supper. She had told Jim that she wanted to have a really nice dinner and a good night's rest before they headed to Switzerland. Jim loaded the gold into the van that was in his garage. He had walked over to his truck. Jim climbed in. He then took out some papers from the glove compartment. Jim started to walk back to the garage. He put his key into the driver's side door of the van, and he opened the door. Jim climbed inside. He then put the forms that he had been carrying in the van's glove compartment. Jim had turned around, and he could not believe what his eyes were seeing.

"Not one word," Kevin said. Agent Kevin Crainey had his weapon drawn. He then told Tom that he would shoot him if he made any sudden move. "So you thought you would get away," Lisa said. She had walked up from behind Kevin. "Let's go inside, and I'll take those keys, Tommy boy," Kevin said. The three of them walked into the house. Donna was in the kitchen, and Kevin told Tom to call her out into the living room. "Nancy, can you come here?"

"Nancy," Lisa whispered. Nancy came out from the kitchen, then she saw Laura and a man with a gun to Jim's head. "Not so fast, Nancy or Donna or whatever name you're using," Lisa said.

"Laura, I don't understand."

"Shut up and sit in that chair!" Lisa yelled. Lisa had her gun pointed at Donna's head. Kevin then tied up Tom and Donna to the chairs they we're sitting in. Lisa had started to mock them. While Kevin went over to their bar, he made himself a drink. He then walked back over toward Tom. "So look what we have here, Agent Allen and his slut girlfriend!" Lisa started to laugh uncontrollably. She had found it very amusing what Kevin had just said. "I can't believe that you actually thought that you would get away from the agency," Kevin said.

Donna looked at Lisa as if she wanted to rip out her eyes. "Don't look at me like that, you bitch," Lisa said. Lisa then went on to tell Donna that she had despised her and that she could not stand working undercover, putting up with her stupidity. Lisa then opened her purse. She took out Donna's engagement ring, and she threw it at her. "This is a gift from your comatose boyfriend." Lisa then started to walk to the bar. She turned around, looked at Donna, and said, "My name is not Laura. It's Lisa!" She then poured herself and Kevin a glass of champagne. The two of them made a toast in front of Tom and Donna, to their newfound wealth. Lisa and Kevin laughed, then they kissed. Kevin went outside, then Lisa walked over to Tom and Donna. She gagged their mouths so they wouldn't speak. Kevin thanked Tom for retrieving his gold. He had just come back from the garage. He was gloating to Tom about how rich he and Lisa were going to be. Lisa had gone into the kitchen to finish the dinner that Donna had started. Kevin told Tom that he had thought about killing him but decided not to because he was once his onetime friend. Kevin also reminded Tom that he and Donna were still fugitives. After he and Lisa left, they would not jeopardize their location, he said. "The two of you can stay in West Germany."

Lisa had finished the dinner that Donna had started cooking. She then set the table. Lisa then lit some candles. She turned off most of the lights in the house. Kevin had complimented her on the fine food that she had prepared. While they were eating, Tom started to make sounds like he wanted to ask them something. So Kevin got up from the table and removed his gag. "What is it?" Kevin said.

"How did you find us?"

"That was easy, Tommy boy. You forgot the journal. I must admit, hiding it in your cat's traveling cage was a stroke of genius." While Kevin was placing the gag back over Tom's mouth, Lisa got up from the table. She walked over to where her purse was. She took out the journal. Lisa then looked at Donna right in her eyes. "Here's your Nazi father's diary. I won't be needing it anymore." Lisa laughed uncontrollably as she threw it on the coffee table. Lisa and Kevin had consumed quite a bit of champagne. Lisa was feeling tipsy. She looked over at Tom, then she started to remember the times that they had made love together. Then she looked at Kevin. Lisa then grabbed his hand. She led him down the hallway to the bedroom. Lisa glanced back at Tom. She gave him a seductive look as to say, "This is what you're missing!"

Kevin and Lisa were having intercourse down the hallway in Nancy's bedroom. Lisa was making quite a bit of noise as she screamed in ecstasy. Jim knew that when Kevin said he wasn't going to kill them, he knew that Kevin was lying. Jim had witnessed when Kevin murdered a suspect. Just before he shot him, he had said, "So long, my onetime friend!" He knew that this would be his only chance to break free. He had started to look around the room. Jim could not believe his eyes. Right next to him was a knife next to a vase with flowers inside. Jim moved his chair a little bit. He maneuvered his hands. He then took the knife, and he started to cut the rope. He quickly freed himself, then he untied Nancy. Jim could hear Lisa moaning like a puppy. He knew that they were still busy. He told Nancy to get the briefcase in the living room closet while he would get the spare keys hanging in the kitchen next to the telephone. Nancy grabbed her father's diary, which Lisa had put on the table.

Nancy then picked up the engagement ring that Lisa had thrown at her. She then picked up Lisa's purse and emptied its contents on the couch. Nancy then placed the ring in the purse and zipped it up. She then sat the purse on the plate of food, which Lisa was eating. Jim and Nancy quickly made their way to the garage; they jumped into the van. Jim started it. He looked at Nancy; she had a smug look on her face. They drove out of the driveway. Jim and Nancy McGonagall now knew that their lives were at stake and they needed to get away.

Kevin and Lisa finally finished. He lay on the bed, exhausted. Lisa had gotten up to go to the bathroom. She looked down the hallway. That's when she could see some items that were thrown on the couch. The closer she got, the more she recognized them. Lisa then noticed that the chairs that Tom and Donna were tied up in were empty. Lisa let out a scream that could be heard around the world. Kevin came running out of the bedroom. He quickly understood what just happened. Lisa saw all her possessions on the couch. She knew that they were from her purse. She looked over and saw it sitting on the dining room table.

Lisa went over to the table. She then picked up her purse. She wiped off some of the food that had stuck to it. She unzipped it, and when she looked inside, that's when she saw the ring. As she took it out, she looked at Kevin. "I'm going to kill that bitch!" Kevin told Lisa to relax, all was not lost yet, but they had to move quickly. Kevin told Lisa to get dressed. She didn't understand, but she did as he said. Soon Agents Kevin and Lisa Crainey were running out the front door. They were headed to their car.

Jim and Nancy McGonagall were driving on the expressway. Nancy had turned around, and she looked at all the cloth bags of gold. She started laughing. "I can't believe that Lisa could be such a witch," she said. Nancy started to open her father's journal; she took out the little flashlight that was in her purse, and she started to read. Jim looked out his driver's side mirror. He noticed that no one else was on the highway. He seemed relieved, so he started to relax a bit.

He put on the vehicle high beams while he accelerated the van. There was no speed limit on the West German highway.

Kevin and Lisa drove to the end of the road leading away from the golf course. Kevin got out of the car, and he looked at the road. He noticed burnt tire tracks heading west. Kevin knew that Tom was headed to the highway. But he had to move fast because there were north- and southbound lanes, and he didn't know which one Tom would choose. "Lisa, turn on the tracking monitor." Lisa picked it up and turned it on. "You bugged the van?" she asked. "Yes, I did!"

"You are a genius, Kevin. That's why I love you." They started to pick up a beep, but it was real faint, and it was coming from the direction of the expressway. Kevin had finally reached the on-ramp, but the monitor was blank, so he decided to head north. Lisa was getting frustrated. They had been driving for two hours, but there was no sign of Tom and Donna. They had decided to stop at the next rest area. They needed to get some gasoline and stretch their legs. The sedan that they were renting was comfortable, but Lisa needed to use the bathroom. Kevin took the rest area exit. As he was pulling into the parking lot, he saw a white van that looked like Tom's. He walked over, and he saw that no one was in it. Kevin put the key that he had taken from Tom into the lock. Kevin tried to unlock the door, but the key didn't fit.

Nancy was getting hungry. She was quite a bit upset at Lisa and Kevin for interrupting her going-away dinner that she was preparing for her honey, Jim. He had agreed with her, so he pulled into a rest area to get some gas and grab a bite to eat. They had been driving for over three hours. Jim knew that he had put some distance between Hannover and where they were. Jim and Nancy McGonagall ate their food. They talked for a while. Nancy wanted to know what their plans were. She told Jim that she had liked the house that they lived in. Nancy had expressed to Jim that she was going to miss the Laiweneeks. Jim reassured her that he had anticipated and he had prepared for any distractions, but he really did not expect to leave the way that they did. Jim also reminded her that Kevin and Lisa would not give up. "Nancy, Kevin is a former Navy SEAL. I have seen the killer instinct in his eyes. Despite what Kevin had told us, he was not about to let us live. He was going to kill us and take the gold. He is now ambitious, consumed with rage, with the desire for wealth. Sweetheart, that makes him a worthy adversary, which we should never ever underestimate, him or Lisa again." Jim had told Nancy to try and get some sleep, that they would continue their journey at first light.

"Jim, I love you." She then smiled at him, closed her eyes, and she fell asleep.

Agents Kevin and Lisa Crainey had slept at the rest area. Kevin woke up. He looked at Lisa, and he tapped her on the shoulder. Lisa responded, and she asked him what time it was. "Its 6:45 a.m." The sun was coming up over the horizon. It was bright and orange. It had looked as if it was going to be a nice day. Kevin had decided that he had driven the wrong way. "How can you tell?" Lisa asked. He ignored her question as he started the car and drove onto the expressway heading north. There was an overpass about a mile up the road, and Kevin wanted to take it. He was now traveling on the southbound lane. There was a little bit of traffic, but the cars were moving pretty fast. "I like how fast people drive here," Kevin said. "When I get my hands on that slut, she's dead!" Lisa yelled. Kevin liked the way Lisa had approached matters. She had rolled down her the window a little bit, and the wind was blowing her blond hair around. He looked over at her. Kevin knew she was his soul mate. "Kevin, why are you so sure that Tom and Donna went this way?"

"Lisa, last night I was dreaming. In my dream, I had a vision of a van full of gold. I needed a place to put it, so I drove to Switzerland, and there I found a Swiss bank."

Lisa then started to laugh. She then punched Kevin on his shoulder. She then told him to stop lying. Lisa had known that he made up the story, but she had understood what he really had meant. Lisa then grabbed his hand, and she started to rub his hand with her index finger.

Jim and Nancy had continued on their way. They had started to drive an hour before sunrise. Jim had soon realized that he and Nancy were almost to the border. He wanted Nancy to be able to practice her new signature and to learn her new identity. Jim had gone on to tell her that just like she did back in New York, she needed to know all of her identification information. There was a sign ahead that said, "Food and lodging." Jim had told her they were going to stop there for a while. When he pulled into the parking lot and parked, Jim looked at her. "Nancy, after I sign in for our room, this will be the last time we can use our current names. From this moment on, Jim and Nancy McGonagall must never be mentioned by us again." Nancy smiled. She bent over toward Jim. She looked him in the eyes. She then told him how much she loved him. Nancy kissed him on the lips.

Jim had rented a room, which he and Nancy settled in. Jim decided to take a shower. Nancy had sat down. She opened up the briefcase. She took out her new passport and some of her documentation papers. She looked at her name, and she then smiled. It said Barbara Marribito.

Kevin and Lisa were making real good time driving. About twenty minutes ago they began to pick up a flashing beacon on their tracking monitor. The more they drove, the faster the red light on the beacon started to pulsate. It had started to get cloudy out. About an hour ago Lisa had commented on how fast the weather had changed. Kevin had to turn on the windshield wipers. It had started to rain. "They must be at the lodging area," Lisa said. Kevin and Lisa had driven past a sign that had told them there was a food and lodging rest area ten miles ahead.

Barbara went in to take her shower. Frank had walked over to the window. He then looked out at the van. He did not like leaving the gold alone. The rain was coming down pretty hard. The rain helped Frank relax a little bit. He opened the emergency suitcase. He was putting on his socks when he'd remembered boot camp and what Chief Petty Officer Davies said: "A good sailor always adapts and overcomes all obstacles placed in his way along life's journey!"

Frank and Barbara Marribito were practicing calling each other by their new names. They were going over their identification numbers. About five minutes before, they had heard the sound of furniture breaking. The couple in the room next to theirs had been auguring; they were screaming and yelling at each other. A few minutes later Frank heard a car door slam and the sound of static coming from a radio. He immediately had recognized the sound. Frank had heard it many times before. He walked over to the window and saw a police cruiser parked beside his van. Frank Marribito looked at Barbara. He then told her to finish getting dressed; it was time to leave.

Kevin drove into the parking lot. He was driving real slowly in front of the motel rooms. "Right there," Lisa said. "Where?" replied Kevin. "See, Kevin, there's the white van parked next to that police car." Kevin drove a few feet away. He then backed up the large four-door sedan. Kevin put the gear lever into park. He turned off the engine. Lisa and Kevin were observing the commotion that was going on. They could see the police officer getting out of his vehicle. "When that slut comes out, then we will take what's rightfully ours," Lisa said.

Frank put the key to their room on top of a fifty West German mark, then he placed the money on the night table. They left the room. They quietly walked to their van. They could see through the door of the room next to theirs because it was open. Barbara looked at the woman who was sitting on the bed crying. She was talking with the police officer. Frank noticed that the man had been standing near the bathroom door entrance. Frank and Barbara climbed into their van; they had started to back out of their parking spot when Barbara said, "Frank, look. Doesn't that look like Lisa?" Frank quickly looked out Barbara's side door mirror. He quickly realized that Kevin and Lisa were parked there. Frank knew that Kevin and Lisa had seen them, but because the police were there, he and Barbara were still alive. "Thank you, God," Frank said. Frank knew that sometimes a little divine intervention was always welcomed. Frank and Barbara quickly made their way back onto the expressway. Kevin had started his car, but when he mashed the gas pedal, their car stalled. He quickly started the car, and they sped off. "Kevin, slow down. We have the monitor." But it was too late as Kevin spun around the corner leading out to the exit of the rest area.

Another police unit was pulling into the rest area when he saw Kevin speeding. He quickly went to pursue. "Give me the tracking monitor," Kevin said. Lisa handed it to him, so Kevin put it under his seat. The police car blasted its siren for them to pull over. "Kevin, I told you to slow down!"

"Good afternoon, Officer," Kevin said while he was rolling down his window.

"License and registration." Kevin handed the police officer their passports and his license. The policeman glanced inside the vehicle. "Mrs. Crainey, you need to remind Led Foot to slow down in residential areas."

"Yes, Officer, I will!" Just as soon as Lisa had finished speaking, the officer got a call over his walkie-talkie. Dispatch was telling him that the situation back at the motel was getting out of control. The police officer quickly handed Kevin and Lisa their documents. He told Kevin to slow down. The officer ran back to his cruiser.

Frank and Barbara had reached the border. It was only a few miles away from the motel. He looked out his side mirror. Frank did not see the large blue sedan. The rain had slowed down to a drizzle. There were a few cars in front of him.

"Frank, how did they find us?"

"I don't know, Barbara."

The Swiss mountains were in the foreground. Barbara could see the snow-covered peaks. "Frank, the mountains, they look so beautiful. They remind me of the White Mountains in New Hampshire when you drive over the hill on the highway." Frank was listening to Barbara, but he had more important matters to attend to. He kept looking through his side mirror at the road behind him. The border guards were checking the vehicle in front of his van. They had a guard dog that was walking around the back of the car. Suddenly, the dog began to bark. "Frank, do you think they will look inside the van?" Suddenly, two more border agents came over to the vehicle. They had their weapons drawn and were telling the occupants to get out of the car. Barbara had a worried look on her face, but Frank told her to act natural. One border guard got into the car. He then drove it over to a waiting area. The other border guard told Frank to pull up, and he did as he was told. The guard asked for their documents while another guard was walking the German shepherd around the van. The border patrol agent gave Frank and Barbara their papers, then he said, "Enjoy your vacation in Switzerland."

Frank and Barbara finally made it past the checkpoint. They were traveling to the Swiss capital. Frank wanted to deposit their gold. Frank looked out at his mirror. He could see Kevin approaching at a very fast rate of speed. Frank was driving on a straight way. He knew that Kevin would soon catch up to him because of all the weight the van was carrying. To make matters even worse for them, the mountains were getting closer by the minute. Frank Marribito knew that he had to climb some of them. "Frank!" Barbara yelled. Frank had been looking out at his mirror when he began to focus on the road in front of him. There were flashing red lights, so Frank looked over to his right. He saw the train approaching at a high speed. He mashed the gas pedal to the floor. The van started to accelerate, then Barbara screamed. The van drove across the tracks just as the crossing guards had started to come down. Frank Marribito looked out of his driver's side mirror. All he could see was sections of train passenger cars crossing over the road.

Frank was driving their van up the side of the mountain. Barbara was telling him how awesome he was. She was still shaking. The adrenaline was still flowing through her body. She had never experienced a near-death situation before. Barbara had wanted to slap him, but she knew that if the train did not kill them, Kevin would have. The road they were traveling on was fairly narrow, and there were many curves. The road was a little slippery from the rain that had fallen earlier. "Frank, turn the heat on, I'm cold." The higher the van climbed up the mountain, the colder outside it had become. Frank was driving at a slow rate speed. There weren't many guardrails on the side of the road. Frank looked out of passenger side mirror as he was driving around the curve, and there was no sign of Kevin and Lisa. There was a fork in the road a few miles back. Frank knew that Kevin would eventually catch up to them. He had hoped that Kevin would go left, because he went right. The blue sign on the side of road had said, "Bern, 40 miles."

Kevin pulled out the tracking monitor from underneath his car seat. He had stopped at the fork in the road. Kevin turned the monitor on. The red beacon light immediately started flashing in the direction pointing to the Swiss capital of Bern. "I knew he was heading for the capital. There are a lot of federal reserve banks there, so, Lisa, we need to catch them before they deposit our gold," Kevin said.

"Slow down, Kevin, the roads are wet!"

"I know, Lisa, but with all that weight Tom is carrying, we can catch up to them."

"Kevin, look, I think that's them going around the curve up ahead."

Kevin continued to accelerate. He told Lisa that they would soon be driving through the valley because they were starting to drive down the side of the mountain. Kevin went on to tell Lisa that the valley would be the best place to kill them and take back their gold.

Frank looked out of his driver's side mirror. He thought he had seen a car. Before he had driven around the last bend, he then started to accelerate the van. "Frank, what's the matter?"

"I'm not sure, but I thought that I saw a car!" Barbara looked out her mirror, and she didn't see any vehicles. The road had come to a straight way. That's when Frank saw the blue sedan. "Don't these two ever give up?" he said. Frank mashed his gas pedal, then the van started to pick up speed. The van was driving into the next curve. Kevin and Lisa were driving right behind them. Suddenly, Frank hit his brakes, then his van spun. He quickly had to straighten up the front end as the rear end began to slide sideways. He continued to wrestle with the steering wheel until the van began to straighten up.

"Look out!" Lisa yelled. Kevin turned his steering wheel as he tried not to hit the pack of mountain goats. The goats were crossing the road, but their car hit one, and the force of the collision caused the large sedan to spin out of control on the wet road, then their vehicle went over the side of the cliff. Frank had straightened up his van, then he locked up his brakes. Smoke from the burning rubber was coming out the back of the van. He and Barbara got out of the van; they had run over to where the car had gone over the side of the mountain. They both looked over the side; they could see the car upside down. The blue sedan was resting on a ledge about seventy feet down the side of the mountain.

"Frank, do you think she's dead?" You could see half of Lisa's body protruding from the passenger's side of the car. "That's definitely her. I can see her blond hair laid out on the rocks," Barbara said.

"Kevin must be pinned inside, his foot is still on the gas pedal," Frank said.

"How can you tell, Frank?"

"See, Barbara, the rear tires are still spinning, the exhaust is still coming out of the tail pipe." Just as Frank finished his sentence, the car exploded into a huge fireball. It then rolled down the side of the mountain. Barbara had screamed because the explosion startled her. A few seconds later, they both had realized what had just happened, then they both became very jubilant, while they hugged and kissed each other. Frank looked back down the side of the mountain. He then said, "So long, my onetime friend!"

"Good afternoon, sir. How may I help you?"

"I have a large shipment of pure gold which, I would like to deposit into my account."

"May I see your credentials?"

"Yes," said Frank.

"Mr. Marribito, welcome to our bank. My name is Otto. I am at your service, sir." Otto summoned some security guards to escort Frank to his van. Barbara then followed Frank and the guards back into the bank. Barbara sat in the bank lobby while Frank followed the security guards and Otto to the elevator. They went inside. Frank noticed how large the elevator was. He looked at the security camera.

He then looked at the control panel. There were six buttons marked below the ground floor. Otto pressed the number four button, then the platform started to move down. When they had reached the fourth level, the doors opened up. Frank noticed a lot of secured vaults. Otto turned right. He then told Frank to follow him. The guard was pulling the gold behind them with an electric pallet jack. They walked down a long corridor until they came into an opening. There were bank employees at the weight station. The employees proceeded to open the bags, and they inspected the gold. They processed the metals. About two hours later, they had the metals in containers, sealed and ready to be stored. Frank sat down in the waiting area. There was a full-length glass window so he could monitor their progress.

Frank saw Otto walking toward the waiting room. He handed Frank a notarized deposit receipt. Frank Marribito looked at the amount and almost fainted. He knew that he was rich when he opened the chest, but he had no idea how much money he would actually receive. Frank shook hands with Otto. Barbara had stood up when she saw Frank walking toward her. Frank had a big smile on his face as they were walking out the bank entrance. Barbara was demanding that he tell her how much money they made. Frank just kept on smiling. They climbed into the van, and Frank looked at her. "Well, just don't stare at me. How much did we make?" Frank reached into his pocket and opened the receipt. He looked at it for a brief moment, then he gave it to Barbara. Barbara could not believe what her eyes were seeing. She yelled, "Six million dollars!" Barbara Marribito had the biggest smile on her face that Frank had ever seen. She was laughing and crying at the same time. She wanted to know where they were going next. She had told Frank that she was hungry. Frank told her that they had a train to catch. When they get on board, they would eat dinner.

Frank and Barbara reached the train station. Frank parked the van in the rear of the parking lot as far back as he could. He stared out the window, then he thought about the last time that he had parked so far away from an entrance. Frank looked up at the sky. The daylight was fading; he then looked over at Barbara. Frank was

HE WAS ABOUT TO BETRAY HIS OATH

remembering that he had given up his career for this beautiful woman sitting next to him. He saw her long black hair and those gorgeous hazel eyes. "Barbara, I love you!" They both kissed and embraced each other.

Frank and Barbara walked up to the ticket booth. "Sir, may I help you?"

"Yes, I would like two purchase two tickets to Rome, Italy."

"Frank, you are just full of surprises. I can't believe we're going to Rome." Barbara was very excited about going to the ancient city of Rome.

They boarded the train. Frank purchased first-class coach tickets. Barbara and Frank were really enjoying themselves for the first time in a long while. They weren't looking over their shoulders. They had been sitting in the diner section of the train after they had freshened up. The couple was having a pleasant meal when Frank began to open up. He had told Barbara that he was in love at one time with another woman.

Frank had told Barbara that the woman he had loved broke his heart while he was in the navy. His ship would make port calls to Naples, Italy. He and his friend Brian would travel up to Rome. Italy was a NATO member, and the Italian people had treated American service personnel very kindly. One time during a visit he had found a beautiful historic Roman Catholic chapel where people got married. He told Barbara that he wanted to marry the woman that he loved there. But when his relationship did not work out, he had given up those ambitions until he walked into the nursing home and he saw her. Frank stood up and walked over to Barbara. He got down on one knee. Frank pulled out of his pocket the most beautiful diamond ring that he could buy back in the city of Hannover. Frank decided to break their covenant for one last time; he looked into her hazel eyes. "Madonna Anne Murphy, will you marry me?" Madonna looked at the ring, tears started to flow from her face, and a bright smile began to radiate from her expression. She then took the ring, she put it on her finger, then Donna looked up. "Yes, Thomas Allen, I would love to be your wife." The two embraced each other as they kissed.

Frank and Barbara had arrived in Rome. They were staying at the Palladium Palace Hotel. The couple had gotten up early to eat breakfast. They left the hotel. Frank wanted to walk to the chapel. It was only three blocks away. It was a beautiful spring day in May. "Do you have the documents?" Barbara asked. Frank opened the small leather briefcase and checked. "Yes, dear!" Frank and Barbara walked into the chapel. They told the priest that they wanted to renew their vows. But they both knew that in God's eyes they were really getting married. The father had asked them for their marriage certificate. Frank had taken all the necessary steps in making sure that he had all the legal forms and documentations. He had given them to the priest. While the priest was reading the documents, Frank silently thanked Becky. He had hoped that all was well with her. Father Bernasconi asked Sister Maria to be a witness. On May 5, 1989, Frank and Barbara Marribito got married. They left the chapel together. The couple started walking. They were holding hands and smiling. Frank hailed a taxi. The two of them got in. "Where to?" the driver asked.

"The Via Del Corso," Frank said. "The via de who?" Barbara said. Frank started to laugh at his wife. He had told her that was a shopping district. They were going to buy some souvenirs.

The couple went shopping. They had purchased several items from various shops and stores scattered throughout the Via Del Corso. They were sitting and eating lunch at one of the fine outside cafés that lined the streets of Rome. Barbara had looked up, and walking toward her and Frank was a couple still a good distance away. Frank had looked up from eating when he noticed his wife's face. She looked as if she was seeing a ghost. "Barbara, what's wrong?"

"There's a couple walking toward us, and they look like Kevin and Lisa," she said with a lump in her throat. Frank turned around, and he froze. He was thinking to himself that they did look like Kevin and Lisa. "It can't be them, Barbara. We watched their car go up in flames." Frank watched while the couple got closer. Then Frank and Barbara started laughing after the two people walked past them. "Frank, you know those two got what they deserved."

"Barbara, we need to get going. I'm going to take you to a country where we can live the rest of our lives in peace without the fear of the past." Frank and Barbara finished their meal. He wanted to get to their next destination, so they took a taxi back to their hotel.

They quickly went up to their room. Frank began to worry he had gotten caught up with the splendor and the magnificence of the ancient city. But when Barbara said that she saw Kevin and Lisa, Frank began to realize that they might be dead. But he knew there could be other agents after him and Barbara. Frank Marribito desperately wanted to get off the continent of Europe as soon as possible. "Hurry up," Frank said. Barbara was in the bathroom. She was freshening up. He wanted to get to the airport. Frank tipped the bellboy after he had loaded their luggage into the trunk of their taxi. Frank told the driver to head to the Di Ciampino Airport.

Frank and Barbara arrived at the airport. They were walking to their terminal. Frank had looked around. He didn't spot anybody acting suspicious, so he reached into his suit pocket, then he pulled out their tickets. Frank then looked at the television monitors. He saw that their flight to Argentina was ready to leave. So he and Barbara headed down the ramp to board their plane. Frank and Barbara were sitting in the first-class section of the airplane. They had some of the most comfortable seats that money could buy.

Frank looked at his wife, and he said, "It sure feels good to be rich." She turned and looked at him. "Promise me that this newfound wealth will not change us."

"Barbara, don't worry, I won't let it!"

Barbara smiled as she laid her head on her husband's shoulder. The captain had leveled the plane. He then eased the flight restrictions. There was a beautiful pair of twin girls around the age of ten a few seats up from them. The girls had on the same outfits, which made them look even more identical. They had started to play a clapping game where they would clap each other's hands simultaneously. The girls were singing a song that they sang in sync with each other as they clapped their hands together. Barbara was watching them, then she said, "Frank, do you want kids?"

"Sure, honey."

Barbara then looked him in the eyes. She said, "The doctor had told me that I have a weak cervix. I might not be able to carry a baby to full term." Frank then told her to pray and ask God for a miracle.

"Barbara," Frank called. She wouldn't answer him, so he called her again.

"Frank, be quiet, I'm praying for that miracle!"

A few minutes later the stewardess was delivering food and beverages.

The stewardess had pulled her cart next to Frank and Barbara. They ordered some drinks and sandwiches. They were really excited about living in South America. Frank knew that in a few short years, he and Barbara would age some. Frank had understood that they would easily blend right into the large European population that inhabits the beautiful country of Argentina. The plane started to vibrate and shake violently. The captain came over the intercom. He announced that they were experiencing some turbulence. Meanwhile in the back of the plane a stewardess was holding on to her meal cart. After a few seconds the plane had calmed down. The flight attendant finished pouring a drink for a passenger. She then pushed her cart up to the next seat. "Sir, would you like something to drink?"

"Yes, ma'am, I'll have a Sprite!" He looked at her chest. Her name tag said Elena.

ABOUT THE AUTHOR

Rodney Searcy resides in the great State of North Carolina. He is currently employed as a Quality Assurance Technician at the largest pork processing plant in the United States, where he oversees the daily production of Pork. He is married to his wife Cynthia, and has two step children Shanquise and Alisha. He enjoys sports, fishing and reading.

CPSIA information can be obtained at www.ICGtesting.com
Printed in the USA
BVOW08s1512201015

423262BV00001B/8/P

9 781682 133613